# THE GRAVE ROBBERS' CHRONICLES

## VOL 5

## Deadly Desert Winds

### BY XU LEI
### TRANSLATED BY
### KATHY M

The Grave Robbers' Chronicles: Volume 5
Deadly Desert Winds
By Xu Lei
Translated by Kathy Mok

Copyright©2014 ThingsAsian Press

Edited by Janet Brown and Michelle Wong
Illustrated  by Vladimir Verano


ThingsAsian Press
San Francisco, California USA
www.thingsasianpress.com
Printed in China

ISBN-13:  978-1-934159-35-4
ISBN-10:  1-934159-35-2

# TABLE OF CONTENTS

UNCLE THREE

## CHAPTER ONE

# UNCLE THREE WAKES UP

Uncle Three was unconscious for over a month after we returned from the palace of doom, but even though he was comatose, I still didn't trust him. I stuck close to his side, sleeping on the next bed, my eyes glued to every twitch he made. The nursing staff thought I was crazy, but they didn't know my uncle the way I did. That old bastard was healthy enough; he just refused to come out of his coma.

"His wounds were terribly infected and your uncle is no longer a young man. Who knows? He may never wake up," his doctor told me.

I waited as patiently as I could, keeping busy by thinking over the details of our latest expedition. Most of all, I was haunted by Qilin's march with the Soldiers of the Dead through the bronze doors, disappearing into a mystery I might never solve. Then there were those two people in the earlier expedition who had disappeared long before we made our way to the burial chamber of their comrades. Had the missing explorers somehow found their way through the bronze doors, never to return?

And why did the undersea tomb lead all who entered it to that damned palace? I looked at my uncle, sleeping peacefully, with all the information I needed locked away in his dreams, and I wanted to kick him.

As I stared at my uncle one morning, his doctor entered the room. "I need to talk to you," he said. "Please come to my office."

"What's the matter?" I asked as I followed him out of the room. Standing in the hallway was one of Uncle Three's shop assistants. "What are you doing here?" I demanded. He stared at me with no reply, and I knew something was up. I rushed back to my uncle's room. His bed was empty.

I heard someone moaning in the hallway. There was my Uncle Three, fully conscious and on his feet, although supported by his older brother, returning to his hospital bed.

Uncle Three had always felt overshadowed by his two brothers. The first, my father, was distant and aloof, Uncle Two was a business success, and Uncle Three? He was a wastrel and ingrate of the first order, according to his older siblings. If he was under the scrutiny of my Uncle Two, I could relax. Uncle Three would be on his best behavior as long as his brother was around.

The three of us sat and chatted like gentlemen instead of grave robbers, uttering no obscenities, curses, or insults. My uncles wanted to know the details of my latest adventure, and I gave them a quick rundown. There were no comments from Uncle Three, who listened impassively, his face twitching only when I told how Qilin had disappeared within the bronze doors.

"Sounds as though both of you have a lot to rest up from—take care of this old man, Nephew," Uncle Two told me as he left.

The minute he walked out of the room, I sprang to my feet and glowered at the source of all my problems. "How long have you been playing possum in this bed? Don't try to tell me about your miraculous recovery that took place the minute I left your bedside and your older brother showed up."

"Don't be disrespectful," Uncle Three muttered. "I woke up because I had to pee."

"For the first time in six weeks?" I demanded. "Oh, forget it. Just tell me why you sent me on that last expedition that nearly killed me, and while you're at it, why did I end up chasing you all over the South China Sea and down into the underwater tomb?"

"None of that has anything to do with you. Just forget it," he told me.

"Nothing to do with me? Then why did you drag me into it? And what about Big Kui, who died on one of your little pleasure jaunts, or Panzi, who is devoted enough that he'd follow you through the gates of hell and back? Shouldn't you show them a little respect and let them know why one died and the other almost did? Not to mention the scars on my back, which I'm sure won't bother your conscience at all, you old devil."

Uncle Three sighed, shook his head, and said, "This matter doesn't concern you, and it would upset you even more if you found out what it was all about. I'm keeping it from you for your own good. Why not leave me in peace?"

"Tell me the truth, Uncle. I'll never give up until I have the whole story, even if I have to haunt every footstep you take until the day one of us dies." I looked him straight in the eye as I said, "You can't wiggle your way out of this, so don't try anything crazy."

Uncle Three let out another deep, long sigh and rubbed his eyes. "Shit, I really never expected this. People say that children are your creditors from your past life, but since I had none of my own, I thought I'd escaped that fate. But here you are, looking for undeserved payment, which you insist on having right this minute."

"You think you owe me nothing? Were *you* almost buried alive in the undersea tomb? Were *you* almost eaten by monkeys near the palace of doom? Were *you*—"

"All right, that's enough, just stop it. I'll tell you, but you have to swear never to tell anyone what you're going to hear from me now. And it's so weird, you may not believe me."

"With what I've seen in the past year, I'll believe anything—just tell me and stop messing around."

Uncle Three pulled half a cigarette left over from heaven-knows-when out of his pocket. He peered into the hallway, saw no nurses, lit up, and took a deep drag. "It was fifty years ago that it started, all because of what your grandfather wrote in the journal. It's a long story. Are you sure you want to hear the whole thing?"

## CHAPTER TWO

# SEARCHING FOR THE DART SUMMIT

I never thought that Uncle Three's narrative would go all the way back to fifty years ago. Although I didn't have Grandfather's journal with me, I could remember the contents very clearly. But since Grandfather didn't write down the ending of his bizarre and terrifying encounter with the blood zombie, we had no idea about what happened after he had lapsed into unconsciousness.

When Uncle Three began to talk, I felt like I already didn't believe him. Grandfather had never breathed a single word about this closely guarded secret to anybody, he and Uncle Three had never gotten along very well, and I was sure my uncle was the last person in whom my grandfather would have confided the mysterious end of his adventure.

"Don't lie to me. Fifty years ago Grandfather was still a kid. And he was so tight-lipped about what happened to him, how would you know anything about it, let alone the truth? Don't just make up a story to fool me. I'm definitely not falling for it."

"When I don't say anything, you get upset. Now that I'm telling you, you won't believe me. What can I do? If you don't trust me then I'm not saying another word. This is all your idea, not mine."

Seeing that he was seizing this chance to shut up again, I hastily apologized. "No, no. I believe you. I'm sorry; I'll shut up. Please go on."

Uncle Three glared at me but resumed his story.

"I can't remember when I first saw your grandfather's journal. It was only after I'd begun my line of work and had heard many weird stories from the older guys. I knew the Changsha grave robbers' saying 'Soil dripping with blood means a corpse dripping with gold.' So when I first saw the journal, I hoped it would help me find something really special, and I read it carefully.

"When I came to the end, I was eager to find this tomb that my father had seen when he was a boy, and had never seen again. I was certain there was treasure there, waiting for me, It was such a strong hunch that I couldn't ignore it.

"My father called the tomb site the Changsha Dart Summit, but that could mean anything; it wasn't specific enough to be useful. I couldn't determine the location of this place, so I let it slide for a while. Then the year before I went with Wen-Jin and the students to the South China Sea, I found some clues.

"I went to my father's childhood home, far in the mountains, in a village that was a four-day walk from any civilized spot. Nobody in the area knew anything about a place called the Dart Summit. I went back home and carefully studied the journal again, piecing what I read together with what I had seen in my father's village and with things I'd heard my father say when I was young. I began to feel sure that the tomb site was in the Mang Shan mountain range so I packed up my gear and set off in that direction.

## 2. SEARCHING FOR THE DART SUMMIT

"I walked for days in the mountains, along a trail that ran along the edge of a cliff. Finally I saw the valley that my father had described in his journal. It was now covered by a lush, green canopy of treetops but emerging through the leaves was a bare red mound of clay, which I was certain had to be the Dart Summit. I also saw something odd standing beside one of the trees near the mound, something that was almost the same color as its forest surroundings but that looked man-made. I took out my binoculars and saw tents, in military camouflage. What were they doing here in a valley where there was little human habitation?

"Then a man walked out of one of the tents. His hair gleamed white against his pink skin; he was quite obviously not Chinese."

## CHAPTER THREE
# THE CAMP

"China wasn't open to the West at that time and few foreigners were allowed in the country. Who was this man and what was he doing here?

"I climbed down the cliff into the valley, found a place to hide my gear, and crept up close to the place where four tents were pitched, right beside the mound of red clay. Nearby a few Chinese sat smoking; they looked like local men hired to carry the equipment. A big bell-shaped pit had been dug on one side of the mound, covered by a bamboo structure that was draped with green canvas.

"Seeing that pit, I knew the foreigners had come for the same reason as I had—to explore the ancient tomb. They had to be archaeologists on a mission sanctioned by the government. And they were doing this all wrong. It was obvious that they didn't know how to dig up a tomb in China.

"That was good, as far as I was concerned. All I had to do was find the right spot, dig a tunnel, and grab everything good before they even began to get close to the tomb. I went back to the spot where I dropped my gear, picked up a shovel, and went off to find the right spot to begin digging.

"I knew the tunnel that had been dug when my father was a boy was bound to have collapsed long ago. I had no idea how far below the surface this group had gone or if they had come close to the tomb. If they had, rain might have soaked through their excavation route and destroyed some of the burial offerings, or even perhaps what had been placed inside the coffin.

"After dark I waited for the men in the camp to go into their tents before I took out my shovel and began to dig. After two hours of solid work, I still hadn't found the right spot. Then my shovel struck something hard. The ground beneath my feet moved and collapsed, my mouth and nose filled with mud, and I plunged into an underground world.

"I landed in a cold pool, with water up to my waist and the smell of rot filling my nostrils. My flashlight was underwater and when I fished it out, the strength of its beam was weak. There was just enough light for me to see that I was in a rectangular room with brick walls. In one of the walls was a hole that looked man-made. That was where I had fallen in, through a tunnel that had its opening covered with dirt to conceal it. Could this have been dug by my own family, half a century ago?

"I thought about this and realized it could have been. Grave robbing was my family business; my skills had been passed down to me by my father, who received his knowledge from past generations. We all used the same strict code of rules and techniques that had been developed centuries ago. All of us would dig the same tunnel in the same spot using the same knowledge and tools. That I would have found a tunnel my father's family had dug was no coincidence.

"I looked around me. My shovel was buried in the avalanche of dirt that had carried me here. It would be difficult to climb back up through the collapsed tunnel, but I had brought some sticks of dynamite with me. I could always blast my way out.

"The rectangular chamber was small with a high ceiling. The water lapping around my waist was dark; I couldn't see if burial objects lay beneath its depths. A door on the left wall looked as though it might lead to a hallway that would take me to the tomb.

"I couldn't tell in which dynasty this tomb had been built, but it didn't hold anybody of noble birth. I figured that out by looking at the height of the ceiling. However, since the walls were made of brick, the occupant of the tomb was at least a government official or someone with a little money. But since royalty wasn't enshrined here, I probably wouldn't have to worry about any traps.

"I began to slosh through the water on my way to the door, trying not to think that I might be stepping on the bones of my ancestors at the bottom of this stinking pool.

"Through the door, the corridor was a short one and I soon reached a larger chamber, with no other passageway leading beyond that. As I came further into the room and approached its center, I saw a coffin raised above the surface of the pool on a stone platform.

"The coffin was open and two rotting bodies leaned against it, their flesh sticking to the stone. I tried not to vomit; could these things be my family? I had learned to think of corpses as nothing more than objects; sentimentality doesn't last long in my line of work, but I'd never before come across bodies that could have been my relatives.

## 3. THE CAMP

"I walked slowly to the platform, my hands shaking so hard that I could barely hang on to my flashlight. When I peered into the coffin I saw only a dried clot of blood wrapped inside fabric that looked like silk. There was no corpse.

"Then I took a closer look at the bodies that leaned against the coffin. They no longer had faces, only skulls. But one held a box gun with two words carved on it— Wu Dagui—my grandfather's name. My knees turned to butter and I knelt before the corpses, bowing twice in respect.

"Then I put on some gloves and reached into the coffin, pressing down on the outside of the fabric. It was indeed silk; beneath it was a mass of slime and a ring-shaped object. It was an iron hoop that encircled the bottom of the coffin.

"I balanced my flashlight on the edge of the coffin and pulled on the hoop with both hands. There was a banging sound and the coffin tilted to one side. Beneath it was a trapdoor.

"Grabbing my flashlight, I raised the trapdoor with my free hand and saw a wrinkled face staring at me.

"I screamed and lost my grip, and the trapdoor slammed shut, smashing into the face. I didn't care if I had hurt it; that thing had scared the shit out of me. What the hell was it anyway?

"It couldn't be a zombie. There was enough fresh air let in after my fall to have turned any zombie back into a corpse. But it might be a blood zombie.

"Changsha is a region with red soil, known as the Land of Blood, and it has many stories of blood zombies. Often when a shovel is plunged into red soil, it comes up dripping with blood, as my father had described in his journal.

"Nobody knows why, although feng shui scholars say that deep burials within red earth, which is what most people want, is where evil spirits dwell. When a dead man is given deep burial, although his children will prosper, eventually his family will all die out. To avoid this fate, many have their children adopted by a family with the same last name before the parent's body is buried.

"The families who sought out deep burial in the red earth of the Land of Blood were usually wealthy and their tombs were full of treasure. Somehow from that stemmed the legend of blood zombies who protected the wealth of the dead.

"Most grave robbers reject all of this as nonsense, which is why my father's grandfather took his son and grandchildren to plunge their shovels into red earth and try their luck. He never expected they would unearth the real thing because he didn't believe those creatures existed.

"Until my father recorded his adventures, there were no written accounts of blood zombies, probably because if one were ever encountered, its victim didn't live to tell the tale. My father was the exception and his account wasn't very clear. He was only a child when this happened, and he was unconscious during part of this episode.

"For my part, I knew it was less important to wonder what had just looked at me or why it was there than it was to figure out how to defend myself against it, or how to escape from it if I had to. All I had to protect myself with was a machete—and some dynamite.

"As I thought, I heard a rumbling sound coming from

**3. THE CAMP**

the coffin and saw the trapdoor being pushed open by something below. I had nothing to lose. I jumped into the coffin and put all my weight on the trapdoor as it opened. A shriveled hand, fingernails twice the length of its fingers and its skin covered with green mold, reached toward me through the small open space. I jumped up and down on the door, hoping to sever the hand, but the damned thing seemed to be made of steel.

"A powerful force pushed the door so hard that I almost fell. I regained my balance and clutched the sides of the coffin with both hands, still pressing down with all my strength. I knew if whatever it was emerged from the trapdoor, I was going to die. My strength was dwindling and whatever pushed on the opposite side was getting even stronger; soon I saw the face peering through the widening crack, staring into my eyes with a horrifying lack of expression in its own.

"I was flat out of luck. I looked down at my waist, looking for a weapon, but all I could find was an empty wine jug hanging from my belt. Then I had an idea.

"To nourish all things under heaven, give them water; to destroy them, give them fire. A Taoist priest once told me that, adding that the best defense against a zombie was to douse it with rice wine, light a match, and set it ablaze.

"I smashed the wine jug against the face that peered out at me. The jug shattered and some wine dribbled onto the countenance. Quickly I lit a match and stretched it toward the drops of wine; as the match moved closer to the face, I could see it more clearly. Before I could set it ablaze, I stopped moving, frozen with horror."

FATS

## CHAPTER FOUR

# THE AWFUL TRUTH

"The face was a bronze color with scaly skin that had peeled away from the bone on the side farthest away from me. Its eyes had no pupils and yet seemed to be staring into my most hidden secrets. And worst of all, I was sure I had seen it somewhere before.

"The match began to burn my fingers, and the hand gripping mine was trying to turn my bones into powder. I had to do it. I threw the match, the face burst into flame, and I was suddenly grateful that the wine I drank had a high alcohol content. White smoke billowed from the flames, the flesh began to melt, and a terrible stench filled the air. I held my breath until the fire died down, leaving behind it only the blackened bones of a skeleton. Whatever had clutched me so tightly had lost its grip.

"Cautiously I poked at the bones with my machete; there was no response. Only after I'd severed the skull from the neck did I begin to feel safe. My legs collapsed and I fell to the floor of the coffin, gasping for breath.

"I tried to think of what that thing could have been. As little as I wanted to, I had to examine it. I lifted the trapdoor and saw the headless skeleton lying below on a slab of stone.

"It had been a male, and a burly one at that. Then I saw something that made my stomach rise up into my throat. This creature had only one hand. The stump of its arm held bullet holes."

My uncle stopped his story and looked at me. We had both read my grandfather's journal. We knew that the disembodied hand that gripped the silk written record of the Warring States period had belonged to his older brother, One-eye.

"You know who it was that I found behind the trapdoor," Uncle Three said. "And the corpses propped beside the coffin were One-eye's father and grandfather."

I asked, "What happened next? Did you go down to the secret room under the coffin?"

"If it had been you, would you have been able to resist going down?"

I grinned, shook my head, and said, "Don't compare me to you. You know what a coward I am; don't make fun of me. Just tell me what you found in the hidden chamber."

Uncle Three sighed and said, "I'll show you something first." He pulled his backpack out from under his bed and handed me a small ivory box.

I examined it carefully. It was an unfinished box from the Qing dynasty that had never been covered with enamel. When I opened it, I found an ugly, black pebble, like the kind often found in gravel piles at construction sites.

"What's this?"

"That's what I took from the chamber," Uncle Three answered.

I looked at the rock again carefully, but could find

nothing special about it. Just as I was about to pick it up, Uncle Three said, "Don't touch it. It's dangerous."

Surprised by his remark, I gave the box back to him and asked, "It seems quite ordinary. Why was it put inside the secret chamber?"

"Don't underestimate that thing. Bringing it out almost cost me my life. As soon as I was certain that the dead monster had once been my uncle, I began to wonder what was within the chamber before me that had the power to destroy a man that way. I had to enter the room and find the answer for myself, even though I knew this was a stupid idea. I made sure my machete and dynamite were tied securely to my belt and raised the trapdoor. There lay a passageway, so narrow I would have to crawl to make my way along it.

"I lit a match and tossed it down the passage; it burned clear and bright, indicating that there was enough oxygen for me to safely enter. I got down on all fours and began to make my way into the darkness. The air was filled with a stink so disgusting that I had to hold my breath. I pulled out my flashlight and saw that the walls around me were made of smooth blocks of black stone.

"After crawling for about ten minutes, I came to a stone wall carved with bas-relief; this was the end of the passageway. How could this be? I asked myself. Was this a path to nowhere? Is this where the silk volume had been left, just lying on the ground?

"As I examined the wall for a hidden doorway, the carving on it caught my eye. It was a figure with a human face and the body of an owl-like bird. The face was huge, its mouth wide open. It was completely expressionless, and it was impossible to tell if it was a man or a woman.

"Its open mouth led to a space just large enough to have held the silk book that my poor dead uncle had clutched in his severed hand. I looked carefully at the other parts of its face; it had four eyes with circular pupils. But the pupils of the top pair of eyes protruded, while those of the bottom pair were sunk inward; as I looked closer I saw there were two dark pebbles inlaid within the pupils of the upper pair of eyes. In the bottom pair the pebbles had been pried out, leaving two round dents.

"I began to understand what was going on here. The two pebbles had been removed, probably by my uncle. But why had he left the two pebbles in the top pair of eyes?

"Something had forced him to stop looting. Something in this place had caused my uncle to stop being human and changed him to a zombie.

"But how? Were the pebbles poisoned? I had just touched them and nothing had happened; what would become of me if I pried one of them out of its socket? I jammed the tip of my machete into the side of the nearest pebble and pulled hard. It dropped into my hand.

"Nothing happened. I pulled at the second pebble. It shot out and fell to the floor before I could catch it, landing with a bang that broke it into fragments. A cloud of dust arose from the pieces. As it filled the air, I began to cough. Then a spicy taste filled my mouth and I was sure it must be poison. I quickly covered my mouth and nose as I stepped back.

"On the ground in front of me where the pebble had smashed to bits was a red worm curled into a ball, making a strange, creaking sound. I'd read about this. It was the

4. THE AWFUL TRUTH

larva of a corpse-eating insect and it was hatching right this second. Worse still, it was a red corpse-eater, much deadlier than any other kind. One touch from this insect would poison me in a heartbeat.

"But I'd also read that these red corpse-eating bugs only lived within dead bodies. How could this one have survived inside a pebble?

"There was no time to think this over. The insect began to crawl about, flapping its wings, ready to take its first flight. Once it took to the air, it would kill me in a second.

"I took two steps back, grabbed my machete, and smashed it down on the corpse-eater with all of my strength. Immediately I heard a creaking sound under my blade; a red shadow flashed out from beneath the steel, and the corpse-eater was on my shoulder.

"There was only one thing for me to do. I hurled my machete, flat side down, onto my shoulder, knocking the insect against the wall. It was still alive, fluttering its wings and emitting a bitter smell as it clicked and clattered like a demented frog.

"I realized it was impossible to kill this thing. My only defense was to get away from it and I began to crawl backward toward the trapdoor as rapidly as I could. My hand trembled as I reached to open the door; it swung open, and as it did I saw a flash of red before my eyes.

"I had developed one talent when I was a boy. I could blow dead coals into flame with one gust of my breath; my lung capacity was almost the strength of a small whirlwind and I put it to the test now. I blew every ounce of air in my lungs at that damned bug; the force of my breath blew it off course, sent it into a somersault, and smashed it into the wall. Quickly I dove through the trapdoor and slammed it shut behind me.

"The corpse-eater was close behind but it was one second too late. I could hear it crash into the trapdoor, clicking violently. I wasted no time, gathered up the bones of my dead relatives, and climbed out of the tomb.

"I found a spot where I could cremate the bones and then I returned home to Changsha, telling nobody where I had been— not even my father. I kept the pebble from the tomb; one night I got drunk at a funeral and began to show it off. The funeral director grabbed it away from me and sniffed at it. -'That's not a pebble,' he said.

"'Right, of course. Then what the hell is it, old man?' I blustered.

"'It's a capsule of immortality,' he told me.

"He said this so solemnly that I sobered up at once. Pulling him away from the rest of the group, I asked him to tell me all he knew. Unfortunately he didn't know much at all, only that it had probably been buried with someone very important.

"I was confused. If this was a capsule of immortality why did its counterpart contain a corpse-eater, which would mean certain death if swallowed? Over the next few months, I found out nothing more about this capsule. It seemed to be such a useless piece of shit that I was tempted to flush it down a toilet. Luckily I didn't do that."

## CHAPTER FIVE
# VIDEOTAPES

"A year or so after I found the strange pebble, archaeological excavations became common and many foreign expeditions came to Asia in hopes of carrying off great wealth. Marine archaeology in China at that time was practically nonexistent. Watching national treasures being scooped up and spirited away to other countries, the Chinese archaeological community grew worried and several professors wrote to the central authorities, requesting government support for local archaeologists. A few Chinese 'expedition teams' were scraped together, and one of them was the group of students that Wen-Jin and I took to Xisha in the South China Sea.

"As we gathered equipment for the trip, one day a student announced that somebody had come to see me. When I went to see who it could be, to my surprise I found it was a distant cousin whom I hadn't seen in years, a man named Jie Lianhuan. Because of our family connection, I had to be polite so I stopped work and took him out to lunch. As we neared the end of our meal, I asked, 'What brings you here? And how did you know where to find me?'

"'I was hoping you could persuade Wen-Jin to let me go

on this expedition with you. Marine treasure has always interested me and I'll never get a chance to be part of an adventure like this again,' Jie Lianhuan replied.

"'Don't try to fool me,' I said. 'You'd never want to do this unless there was something in it for you. What is it?'

"'I can't tell you all of it, but there is this: I have a client who wants me to take a look at whatever you may find. All he wants is information and because of the conflict between China and Vietnam in this area of the South China Sea, I can't get out there on my own.'

"I knew the only way I could find anything more would be to let my cousin tag along and then watch him as a starving cat would a bird. 'I'll do what I can for you,' I told him.

"As soon as Jie Lianhuan left, I hired some local guys to follow him and see what he was up to. They told me my cousin had met a foreigner and was talking to him in a tea shop but they had no idea why. So I went to see for myself.

"Sure enough, Jie Lianhuan was with an old foreigner, a sturdy-looking man with silver-white hair, who looked oddly familiar to me. As I stared, I realized he had been the foreigner I spied on at the Dart Summit the year before, at the tomb of the blood zombies."

My uncle fell silent and I mumbled something in surprise. Somehow this old foreigner had known about the undersea tomb; he was the reason Jie Lianhuan had begged to go on Wen-Jin's expedition. How did this old man know about the cave of the blood zombies and the undersea tomb too? When Jie Lianhuan's corpse was found, he had a bronze fish with snake brows in his clenched fist. Was that what the old foreigner had sent him to find? And how the hell did this old man know so much?

Then I stared at my uncle with murder in my heart. Was he lying to me again?

"Uncle Three, stop the bullshit. None of this can be true."

"What are you talking about?" he asked, and I told him what I'd been thinking.

"It's not as simple as you make it out to be," he said quietly. "The foreigner had no idea of what was under the sea at Xisha. He only suspected there might be something there that he wanted. He told me himself later; he's one of the owners of the company Ning works for. And he's the American who swindled your grandfather out of the silk book that came out of the tomb. I met him once; he's on life support now and since he'll soon be dead, he told me what his story was. This old man deciphered the text of the silk book—and you'll never guess what it said—"

He was interrupted by a knock on the door of his hospital room; it was an express courier asking for Mr. Wu. "There's a package for you," he said. It had my name on it, so he handed it to me and left.

"Who is it from?" my uncle demanded.

I turned it over and read the sender's name—it had been mailed by Zhang Qilin only four days earlier. I tore open the box—it held two videotapes.

How could Qilin have sent me a package only four days ago when I had seen him march through the mysterious bronze doors with the Soldiers of the Dead? How had he managed to get out and return? And why had he sent me videotapes? Could they reveal what lay behind the bronze doors? How would that be possible? When he had marched into oblivion, he certainly wasn't holding a video camera.

I carefully examined the exterior of the tapes, looking for a message or any sort of label that might be written or glued upon them. There were traces of a label that had been ripped away, and not too long ago either. Why hadn't Qilin wanted me to see it? What was he hiding from me now?

I cursed in disgust, "Damn it. I'm tired of you secretive bastards."

"What the hell are you talking about?" my uncle responded. "You're the one who didn't tell me this poker-faced weasel was back in the world again. When did he come back through the bronze doors and how did he survive his march with the Soldiers of the Dead?"

"I wish I could tell you—but even more important is how did Qilin know I was here in this hospital?"

"Does the postmark say where the package was sent from? Is there a return address?"

We both peered at the outside of the package; there was no information except Qilin's name and the date the box was put in the mail. It had been sent by express mail and it still took four days to arrive, so it must have been posted from a faraway spot. I would need to check a computer to see which provinces were four days away by express mail.

"Don't worry about problems we can't solve right now," my uncle ordered. "Let's find a VCR and see what's on these tapes."

"No. Not until you finish the story you were telling me. If you stop now, I may never hear the end. Besides, VCRs and videotapes are old-fashioned now. We'll probably need to go to a flea market to find anything that will show us what's on these things."

"You're right. I'll send my salesclerk out to hunt one down.

**5. VIDEOTAPES**

Now back to the story—where was I? Oh, right—the contents of the silk book. Tell me, Nephew, what do you know about the silk books of the Warring States period of history?"

"Not much," I admitted.

"Look at this." Uncle Three held out a photograph. "This is a picture of what my one-eyed uncle found before he died. I took this photo when I was in New York a few years ago, at the museum where the book is being displayed. This thing has cursed our family for four generations; I never wanted you to be ensnared by it as well—I wanted the whole mess to stop with me. But here we are."

"So what the hell is written on it?"

"Nothing, no words, the information is contained in a mysterious pattern. The foreigner told me all about it and now I'm going to tell you."

## CHAPTER SIX

# JUDE KAO

"The old man had been in China long enough to have been given a Chinese name, Jude Kao. He had been a young missionary at a school in Changsha, one of the Americans who came to China when the Kuomintang was in power, but he was more interested in profits than he was in Christianity. He believed valuable archaeological discoveries were no more than commodities to be purchased, exported, and sold for a high price, so he began to smuggle cultural treasures out of the country when he was only nineteen years old.

"There were two types of smuggling businesses at that time: One was the high-turnover operation, where the quantity of goods smuggled was large, but the value was low—a high-volume, high-risk business. Jude Kao preferred high value and low volume, which was much safer. My father, your grandfather, liked that way of doing business too, so he and Jude Kao joined forces.

"But Jude Kao never thought your grandfather was his equal or even someone to respect; in fact he called my father the Bedbug behind his back.

"In 1949, Changsha was liberated and missionaries were told to withdraw from China and return home. Jude

Kao was ordered to leave so he began to close down his business, transferring his assets to the United States. At the last minute he decided to buy as many tomb treasures as he could find. Exploiting his long-standing business relationships and the trust that his Chinese associates had in him, he began to give small advance payments for valuable burial objects, saying he would pay the rest of what he owed and more after selling the treasures in the West. Of course he never paid another penny for what he took away with him—which included your grandfather's silk book.

"Your grandfather didn't want to sell what his brother, father, and grandfather had sacrificed their lives to discover, but Jude Kao lied, saying he would use part of the profits to start a charity that would bring honor to our family name. Your grandfather agreed to let the silk book go and then the real trouble began.

"Jude Kao, to ensure your grandfather could make no trouble for him in the future, sent a telegram to the People's Liberation Army in Changsha, accusing his business associates of being grave robbers. Almost all of the men who had worked with him were executed or sent to prison. Your grandfather managed to escape, hiding in the mountains, but his reputation was demolished. Eventually he left Changsha to live in Hangzhou, never to speak of the silk book again.

"After Jude Kao went back to the United States, he auctioned off the treasures he had swindled from his associates and he made a fortune. The silk book was sold to New York's leading art museum for a very high bid, making him a millionaire several times over.

**6. JUDE KAO**

"Now that he was wealthy and leisured, Jude Kao began to study Chinese culture. His goal was to decipher the contents of the silk book, which was written in a pattern of symbols—not language. Finding an elderly Chinese scholar in New York's Chinatown, he learned that the old gentleman was familiar with this pattern and had once seen the exact same thing carved on an alchemist's furnace in a Taoist temple on Mount Qimeng in Shandong.

"Although it was impossible for Jude Kao to return to China, he was wealthy enough to hire men who could find this furnace for him. So he put out the word that he needed someone with a brain but no conscience, and he found my cousin, Jie Lianhuan.

"It always puzzled me why Jie Lianhuan agreed to work with Jude Kao. It was a dangerous job; smuggling cultural treasures out of the country meant death for those who were caught. Only the very stupid or the very poor would take this sort of risk, and my cousin was neither. How did his name ever come to the attention of Jude Kao? The answers to these questions would remain a mystery to me for years; I wouldn't learn the truth until after my first trip to the undersea tomb.

"Jude Kao sent careful and detailed instructions to Jie Lianhuan, a sketch of the furnace provided by the elderly scholar, and the most advanced camera on the market. He told my cousin to find out if the Taoist temple still existed or if it had become a casualty of the Cultural Revolution. If it was still intact, he needed to go there, take photos of the furnace, and send them to the U.S. for confirmation. If it was truly authentic, then they would need to smuggle it out of China.

"Jie Lianhuan found the temple and its furnace, took photos of both, and sent them back to his employer. Jude Kao was excited to see that the old scholar had been correct. The drawing on the furnace was exactly the same as the one on the silk book. He immediately told Jie Lianhuan to get the furnace out of the country and to New York. This was impossible, both because of the size of the furnace and the government's crackdown on smuggling artifacts of any kind. So Jude Kao came up with an insane idea: he told my cousin to smash the furnace into forty pieces, wrap them in bundles of silk, and send them to New York.

"Without coincidences there would be no stories. When Jie Lianhuan was sawing up the pieces of the furnace, he discovered a clue to the secret of the silk book which allowed Jude Kao to decode its meaning."

Uncle Three stopped talking, took out two crumpled photographs from his backpack, and handed them to me. The first was a picture of a huge alchemist's furnace, almost as tall as I was, on display in a museum. The second photo showed the base of the furnace, where cast in the middle was a bronze animal of some kind, about the size of my fist, staring up at the sky.

"This is the restored furnace at the museum, and the other picture shows its bottom," Uncle Three explained. "Look closely at the pattern around the animal."

The photo was very small. Peering at it closely, I could see many tiny embossed points around the skyward-looking beast.

"This is?" I asked.

"That embossment at the bottom of the furnace is an ancient star chart."

"It's a map that marks the location of the stars in the sky?"

Uncle Three nodded and took out a photo of the pattern from the silk book of the Warring States period so I could compare. "And it's incredibly ingenious. Here's the star chart at the bottom of this furnace. When the lid of the furnace is rotated to the right angle, the curved lines on this drawing overlap with the six stars in the star chart, making a full picture. But the mystery continued—what did the star chart convey to those who had constructed this code? It was so carefully hidden that it had to be very important. To find the answer, first Jude Kao overlapped the chart with the drawing in the silk book and identified the constellations within the picture. Then he turned to ancient astrology books, trying to discover what this constellation chart meant.

"Unfortunately, ancient Chinese astrology was heavily intertwined with feng shui. It was extremely complex, and it was impossible for someone who wasn't a scholar in the discipline to find out the secret concealed in the constellation chart. The only way to solve the mystery was by asking experts in Chinese astrology, but Jude Kao could find none in the United States. So he hired Jie Lianhuan again to make inquiries in China.

"Yet Jie Lianhuan failed to come up with anything. In that era, those who knew a little about these ancient matters were more or less confined to the cowshed. Those who escaped capture didn't dare to reveal their knowledge.

"Driven to despair, Jude Kao suddenly came up with yet another idea. He focused his attention again on the silk books of the Warring States period. Since the star chart was in the silk book, he speculated that there would be records of the secret in other volumes of that time period.

"He began to purchase volumes of the Yellow Silk Book of Lu, and that brought his attention back to my father. There couldn't be just one volume. If my father had stolen one, Jude Kao was sure that he probably had found the whole collection and still had them in his possession.

"By now the relationship between Jie Lianhuan and Jude Kao had grown very strong, and my cousin agreed to get more information from my father. He soon discovered that it was impossible to get a word out of the old man so he came to me. We had a few drinks and I told him everything my father had written in his journal."

"Uncle Three," I interrupted, "were you the one who gave Jude Kao the information about the tomb at the Dart Summit?"

"I was so drunk I couldn't remember a word I'd said once I sobered up. It wasn't until Jude Kao told me later that I was his source of information that I knew what I'd done.

"After Jude Kao received the news, he planned to re-excavate the ancient tomb in the cavern of the blood zombies. Unfortunately Jie Lianhuan didn't know how to rob a grave, and he couldn't find anyone else to do it. The old man had to assemble a group of archaeology students from the U.S. and put together an expedition to go to Changsha, which is where I saw him.

"After I escaped from the ancient tomb that night, Jude Kao went in the next afternoon. Needless to say, the whole thing turned out to be a huge disaster. When they opened the secret trapdoor at the bottom of the coffin, the red corpse-eating insect killed almost everyone, with only Jude Kao and Jie Lianhuan making it out alive.

"A year later, he sent Jie Lianhuan to me and we set off for the waters of the South China Sea."

My uncle's story amazed me and I believed him at last. But there were still a few things that I wasn't sure about.

"Listen," I said, "Jude Kao and Jie Lianhuan had been in contact for years. The meeting that you witnessed was just a reunion. Jude Kao found Jie Lianhuan again and hired him to infiltrate Wen-Jin's Xisha archaeological expedition team, enter Wang Canghai's undersea tomb secretly, and take something out for him. And this was probably the bronze fish that held the secret of the Xia Emperor. Also, according to you, what started all this was the silk book of the Warring States period, but what connection was there between Wang Canghai in Xisha and that book? What made Jude Kao turn his eyes to Xisha?"

Uncle Three nodded. "It was indeed Jude Kao who asked Jie Lianhuan to infiltrate the archaeological expedition team, but your guess is only half-right. In his own words, he didn't ask Jie Lianhuan to enter the ancient tomb for the bronze fish. He only wanted a photograph of the body in the coffin.

"As for why he wanted Jie Lianhuan to do that, the old man wouldn't say, nor would he tell me where he got the information about Wang Canghai's undersea tomb. When I pushed him for an answer, he only offered an old Chinese saying, 'The hidden design of fate must not be disclosed.'"

## CHAPTER SEVEN

# FOLLOWING THE STARS

"Somehow," Uncle Three said, "when Jude Kao was deciphering the code of the silk book, he found something that was connected to the Xisha tomb. Maybe he found someone who helped him break the code—someone who had been to Wang Canghai's underwater burial spot and sent him in that direction."

"What makes you so sure that it was a person who turned his attention to Xisha?" I asked.

Uncle Three replied, "Because his information was so specific and accurate. The only way he could have those details was if he heard them from someone who had already been to the undersea gravesite."

I nodded. What he said was convincing, but why would there be any relationship between the star chart in the silk book of the Warring States period and an ancient tomb of the Ming dynasty? Could someone have seen the star chart and then predicted that a thousand years later a tomb would be built at the bottom of the South China Sea? This was too far-fetched for me to swallow.

And then there of course was the incident in which everyone in Wen-Jin's archaeological expedition disappeared except for Uncle Three. Qilin had shown me evidence that pointed clearly to Uncle Three having killed them all. However, judging from my uncle's expression and behavior as he told me what he knew, he seemed as bewildered as anybody else—and sad too. The whole thing remained a gigantic mystery, with the "truth" depending on what Uncle Three had to say.

After taking a deep breath, my uncle continued. "I'll be straight with you. There are some things about Xisha that I lied to you about. Please understand, this is very painful and it's hard for me to put into words. When I led Wen-Jin and the others to 'discover' the undersea tomb, that was an act; I'd already gone down there with Jie Lianhuan, right to the center of the tomb. Jude Kao had given my cousin directions to the room where Wang Canghai's coffin was."

"You mean the middle of the three chambers?" I asked as I thought about the structure of the undersea tomb.

Uncle Three shook his head. "No. The place you're talking about is only the first layer of the tomb. The vastness of that sunken mausoleum is beyond your imagination. Wang Canghai's coffin is deeply buried in the very bottom layer, in a place that is almost impossible to describe. But Jie Lianhuan had been provided with an underwater flash camera—the most advanced camera in the world at that time, so he could provide a visual description for his employer.

"I knew my cousin was involved in something big and I stuck to him like a blood-sucking leech. Jie Lianhuan was like a ticking time bomb and I wanted to be around when he exploded into action. That night when everyone else was asleep, I heard him get up and I followed him to the deck of our boat. He was launching a kayak and I leaped in beside him before he could row away. At that point he had to tell me where he was going and who had sent him. As he told me everything, the sky turned black, the moon disappeared, and I laughed. 'We are blind men now and you know the old saying. When two blind men enter a cave, one is going to stay there forever. One of us will never come back unless we're both very, very careful.'

"This wasn't a threat, just my way of trying to gain the upper hand, but Jie Lianhuan wasn't falling for that. He smiled back at me without saying a word and led the way into the tomb's opening in silence.

"It's extremely dangerous to dive into an underwater cave within a coral reef, but since we didn't know what we were doing, we had no fears. As we swam through a maze of tunnels I left my mark at each intersection so I could find my way back if I returned alone.

"Half an hour later we swam into a strange and bewildering place, a huge pit. Beneath us was an abyss."

"Draw me a sketch of what you saw," I demanded, and my uncle scribbled a drawing that helped me see where he had been. It was as he said, a gigantic cave within the reef with its exit at the very top of the cavern.

"After we entered this space, there was no passageway to lead us forward," Uncle Three continued. "Nothing on either side, nor in front, and nothing beneath our feet. It was like floating in outer space. Our flashlights became swallowed up in darkness and our oxygen consumption was higher than it should have been. But Jie Lianhuan wasn't worried. After circling in the water for a few times, he motioned for me to turn off my flashlight and he did the same.

"After the two lights went out, darkness covered our vision like a veil of ink. At the same time, a ring of fluorescent paint on the handles of our flashlights slowly took on a glow, so we could each see where the other one was.

"In the darkness below our feet, I could vaguely see a large round mass of green spots, like eyes in the water. I started groping for my knife. But then I saw my cousin's light move toward these green specks and I followed.

## 7. FOLLOWING THE STARS

"The spots of light moved rapidly ahead of us as we plunged forward into the freezing dark water. I grabbed my cousin to pull him to a stop, certain that what we chased were sea monsters, luring us to our death. As we came to an abrupt halt, Jie Lianhuan turned on his flashlight. A stream of white light pierced the blackness, revealing a white object with a human shape. It was a corpse covered in floating white gauze, looking like a flower from hell."

## CHAPTER EIGHT
# THE FLOATING CORPSES

I had to force myself not to swim away as fast as I could. After all, we'd entered a tomb—of course we were bound to come across a few corpses. And sure enough, we had found a matched set, side by side, each draped in white cloth—and beyond those two were even more—at least forty of them. They floated toward us as though they were swimming; whatever the green spots had been were no longer visible under the beam of my cousin's flashlight.

"I looked at Jie Lianhuan. His face was a mass of panic and sheer terror. Obviously he hadn't bargained for this and I felt a rush of rage that he had led me here without any planning or forethought.

"As the corpses came closer, I could see that they hadn't completely rotted away; they still had facial features, and their bodies all held different poses. Some held trays, others played flutes. Although the white cloth that enveloped them moved, their bodies didn't, remaining as stiff as planks of timber.

"And then I realized what we were looking at. I dove down another ten feet or so. These corpses were arranged as though they were part of a famous mural, the Painting of the Dancing Celestial Masters that is found on the walls of the most important tombs. But the occupant of this tomb used real bodies, not painted ones, to send him into heaven. If we followed these corpses, we were sure to find the tomb we were looking for—if we didn't use up all the oxygen in our tanks first.

"We had to go back and get more oxygen or we'd join the band of corpses. I motioned to Jie Lianhuan but he continued to swim toward the bodies, ignoring me. I couldn't abandon him; he was part of my family. I had to go after him; I had no choice."

I peered into my uncle's face as he paused in his narrative. If he felt such a familial responsibility, why did he eventually let his cousin die in the tomb? Were the words that Jie Lianhuan had written in blood on the tomb's wall true? Had my uncle killed this man? Was I listening to the lies of a murderer?

And then Uncle Three burst out with a torrent of words, so rapidly that it took all of my concentration to follow his story.

"I raced to keep up with Jie Lianhuan but he had no intention of letting me catch him. He was a stronger swimmer and I soon fell far behind. As I paddled onward, I was surrounded by broken pieces of carved windows and wooden beams, all encrusted with white salt, and in the middle of this debris was a huge black shadow. The dancing corpses headed straight toward this shape and with them went my cousin.

"It was the bow of an enormous ship, bigger than anything I had ever seen, covered with layers of white sea salt and scablike coral, looking like the skull of a colossal marine monster. The corpses floated into it, followed by my cousin—and me too. Although the ship was encased in rust and its masts looked as though they would collapse if one of us sneezed, Jie Lianhuan and I were speechless as we looked at it. Who could have been interred in a tomb as elaborate as this?

"Before us were jade doors revealing an interior that tempted us both. We swam forward, through the doorways and down a long corridor. Along the walls was a long line of dancing corpses, stretching as far as I could see. At the end of the corridor was a stairway and as I swam up its length, I was amazed to find that my head was no longer underwater and I could breathe easily. Ahead of me Jie Lianhuan was gazing around in a chamber that lay at the top of the stairs, and I joined him.

"We were standing in a room made of brick, typical of tombs built during the Ming dynasty. In the middle were large burial lamps made of blue and white porcelain and a gigantic black iron vat that towered above our heads.

"I could tell this wasn't a royal tomb, but obviously it contained a man who was enormously wealthy. It would have taken tens of thousands of workers to create this burial spot. Who could have afforded this? The richest man of that time would have been hard-pressed to come up with the fortune this would have cost. My cousin had led me to a discovery that would let me live in luxury for the rest of my life.

"I stared about and noticed the murals that embellished the walls of the chamber, strangely unfaded by time. Jie Lianhuan was completely absorbed in staring at them, while I kept a close eye on him. He looked exhausted, as though he had depleted all of his energy just to get here.

"I checked the levels of our oxygen tanks. Mine was still in good shape but my cousin had less than half a tank left. With a shudder of horror, I realized there was no way this man was going to make it out alive.

"The two of us walked to the edge of the chamber. I stopped to examine the huge vat. It weighed easily more than five tons and was covered with carved inscriptions. Something that looked like a fish had been embossed inside at the bottom of the vessel.

"I was trying to read one of the inscriptions when I heard my cousin's voice. He had come to the end of the chamber, and before him was a burial platform holding a massive black coffin. As he let out a muffled shout, Jie Lianhuan backed away from the coffin and I went over to see why.

"With one glance, I backed away too. There was a person lying on the top of the coffin."

8. THE FLOATING CORPSES

## CHAPTER NINE
# THE WHISTLE COFFIN

"I reached for my knife, but as I looked more closely, I saw that what looked like a human body was a bronze statue resting on the top of the coffin. Its limbs were thick and short and its mouth was wide open, as though frozen in a silent scream.

"There was no other coffin to be seen, so this had to contain the tomb's occupant. I went closer and found the whole thing was made of cast iron. The statue's open mouth was a hole that looked as though it led straight inside the coffin.

"'Something's wrong here,' I muttered. 'This looks like a Whistle Coffin, damn it.'

"The 'Whistle Coffin' is something I heard about from my father that isn't an ancient legend; it came into being just before the Liberation period. Zhang Yancheng, a warlord leader who was a follower of Sun Yat-sen, was the man who invented this. He was a king among grave robbers, a man whose powers were almost magical. His left hand had abnormally long fingers that were all the same length which he used to test soil that might contain graves, and the number of tombs he uncovered was phenomenal. While he was alive there was a popular saying, 'Yancheng arrives, the devil jumps, and the King of Hell changes his plans.'

"This man had a special technique when it came to grave robbing. When he uncovered a coffin on ground that was possessed by a malignant spirit, he would drench it with cattle blood and then waited to see what would happen. If an unearthly sound came from the coffin, then the body inside had probably lost all its power. The coffin could be removed from the tomb, left in full sunlight for hours, and then opened. If there was no sound at all, then special measures were needed because what was inside the coffin was something indescribable and demonic.

"Under those circumstances, Zhang Yancheng would order his men to dig a trench, lower the coffin into it, then cover it with a thick layer of mud, followed by a seal of molten lead. Only a hole the size of a man's arm would be left open, leading into the interior of the coffin. When the lead became solid again, Zhang Yancheng would plunge his arm through the opening and into the coffin, removing any object that gave the occupant its evil power. Because of that hole, which the soldiers felt resembled a huge iron whistle, this became known as the 'Whistle Coffin.'

"What I was looking at now looked as though it might be one of Zhang Yancheng's inventions. But why? Could this coffin contain a monster, not a human corpse? Is that why it had been buried at the bottom of the sea? I felt more curiosity than I did fear, longing to open the lid and find the answers to my questions. Jie Lianhuan apparently felt the same way because he rushed over, clumsily pushing at the coffin lid.

"'Stop!' I barked. 'You don't know what you're doing

or what's inside. We need to reach through this hole in the statue's mouth, the way Zhang Yancheng used to.' I climbed up and directed the beam of my flashlight into the hole on the lid.

"Although I saw nothing, my neck tightened as I looked into the darkness. I could feel a horrible power come from this coffin and the last thing I wanted to do was stick my hand into it.

"I climbed back down and began to think. Jude Kao knew so much about this tomb that I was sure he had sent someone in here before, someone who found the Whistle Coffin and knew better than to touch it. So Jude Kao sent my cousin, who didn't know any better, to find out what was inside. My responsibility was to keep Jie Lianhuan from doing anything stupid, without looking like a coward myself. The problem was I really wanted to open it too.

"I thought about what my father would have done. He wouldn't have gone near that coffin without careful preparations. He would have examined the tomb for other treasures and he would have gone to get the right tools, returning to cope with whatever might be inside the coffin.

"'Take photos of the outside of the coffin but don't touch it,' I ordered Jie Lianhuan. 'I'll look around for whatever might be worth taking away with us.'

"Other than the large porcelain lamps, which today would be worth around three billion dollars, I saw nothing valuable. I moved behind the coffin, examining the walls. They were carved in bas-relief, and those carvings were worth a lot.

"They were images of seven palaces, each one different from the next, placed in the arrangement of the Big Dipper. They were set in a mountain valley that was covered with clouds and mist, with a looming mountain above them.

"What do these carvings mean? I wondered. All the murals and carvings in ancient tombs had significance, either symbolic or historical. Were these offering a clue to who was lying in the coffin? They fascinated me. If I could have carried them out, I would never have sold them; I'd put them in my bedroom to stare at every morning when I woke up.

"But it was impossible to carry them out of here. I called to my cousin to come and photograph them but he ignored me. Then I smelled something burning. I ran back and saw Jie Lianhuan standing on top of the coffin. Thick clouds of smoke billowed from the mouth of the bronze statue.

"I raced over and grabbed Jie Lianhuan's arm, pulling him away from the smoke. 'What the hell is going on?'

"'I…I,' he stammered and raised his hands toward my face. He was holding a matchbox.

"'You stupid bastard. You couldn't wait, could you? You had to light a match and throw it into the hole to see what would happen next. You've probably destroyed anything valuable, including any clues as to who was buried in there. God help us help both if any other grave robbers find out about this—we'll never work again, you moron. Where's your canteen?' I grabbed my own water container and poured it into the hole. The smoke still billowed up in clouds.

**9. THE WHISTLE COFFIN**

"'Give me your damned water bottle,' I bellowed. I grabbed it and when I poured the liquid in through the hole, flames shot up toward us as though I'd fed the fire with kerosene.

"'I forgot to tell you,' Jie Lianhuan quavered, 'I had whiskey in my canteen, not water.'

"The flames shot higher as we stood helplessly watching; then my cousin leaped forward, unbuckling his belt. Kneeling on the coffin, he began to urinate into the flames. The smell almost made me puke. This was beyond a doubt the most disrespectful, barbaric action I'd ever seen any grave robber do. This jerk is a disgrace to every ancestor we ever had, I muttered to myself.

"But it worked. The flames died down; the smoke cleared. Jie Lianhuan zipped up his pants and collapsed onto the coffin. Whatever is in there, I thought, has every right to be pissed off.

"I stared at the coffin but nothing moved. No sound came from it. Perhaps there was nothing inside but a few bones after all. Perhaps we could open it and take a few treasures back up with us to show Wen-Jin and the others.

"I climbed back up on the coffin and plunged my arm through the open mouth of the statue. It had only been inside the coffin for a few seconds when I could feel my arm get hotter and hotter. I clamped my teeth together and pushed my arm in further; my fingers began to grown numb, but not as numb as I would have liked. When my hand touched the corpse, it was sticky and disgustingly slimy. I could feel its mouth and when I reached inside I could feel Jie Lianhuan's damned match. It was still burning.

"Then I touched something hard and circular and cold. I clutched it and tried to slip the object out of the corpse's mouth and up through the hole into the open air, but it was too heavy. As I pulled without any success, I felt the entire coffin shake. The sound of creaking metal came from the floor beneath it. Holy shit, I thought, this is a trap.

"A loud rattling noise seemed to be coming from the huge cast-iron cauldron in the middle of the chamber. I snatched my arm out of the hole and turned my flashlight toward the sound. I started to walk toward it, calling for Jie Lianhuan to follow me.

"Above the cauldron were two massive steel chains that hung from the ceiling of the chamber all the way into the interior of the gigantic pot. Something seemed to be attached to the ends of the chains. What the hell is this, I wondered.

"I climbed to the edge of the cauldron and looked inside. There were two large clasps lying at the bottom with a skeleton attached. Its head was much larger and longer than that of a normal human, its arms and legs were missing, and what was left of its body was covered in bronze leaf. The clasps were firmly attached to its collarbones. This was done only to prisoners who were experts in martial arts and would have escaped ordinary shackles.

"The skeleton must have been suspended above the cauldron centuries ago, designed to fall once the trap in the coffin was activated. Clever trick, but what was it for? It was frightening but not lethal. And the skeleton wasn't a normal body—what the hell had it been when it was alive? Obviously it had been very strong and well versed in martial arts, judging by its collar clasps.

"I climbed into the cauldron to get a better look at the bones, telling my cousin that I wanted him to get some photos. He didn't answer but that didn't concern me, especially when I slipped and fell as I tried to climb into the pot. I plunged directly into the arms of the skeleton; the force of my fall shattered most of its bones, including a large part of its skull. I could see into its cranial cavity; within it was a honeycomb-shaped object holding tiny insect eggs that looked like almost translucent gray pearls. When I poked at them with the tip of my knife I found they weren't squishy but hard, as though they had dried up. Why were there so many of them in this man's brain? Were they some kind of parasite?

"Wen-Jin had often talked to me about how she longed to make a significant discovery that no other archaeologist had ever seen before, and I loved Wen-Jin so I decided to take her this cluster of eggs. Maybe it wouldn't make her famous but it would certainly make her love me more.

"Carefully I put the broken skull and its contents into my salvage bag and then climbed out of the cauldron to find Jie Lianhuan. The minute I went back to the coffin I knew something was terribly wrong. My cousin had disappeared; only his flashlight was still here, flickering as it illuminated a nearby mural.

"I'd seen this happen far too many times. When someone went missing, somehow their flashlight always was found lying in the dirt. Had Jie Lianhuan set off a trap when I was in the cauldron? I'd heard nothing, but deep inside that gigantic piece of cast iron, my ears would have been muffled.

"I walked to the opposite side of the coffin and there was Jie Lianhuan, curled up in a ball on the ground, facedown, not moving a muscle. When I pointed the flashlight at him, there was no response. I swept the area with the beam of light but saw nothing.

"I tried to pull my cousin to his feet but he was unconscious and as heavy as a corpse. I checked his pulse; it was normal, but when I touched the back of his neck, it was feverishly hot. I turned him over and saw he was covered with blood. He looked as though somebody had beaten him senseless, but there was no other person here, and a demon or a zombie would have killed him outright rather than battering him into a coma.

"As I tried to make sense of what I saw, the air suddenly turned cold, as though a door had been opened. My mouth turned dry and I grabbed the handle of my knife. Was there another person in this place?"

## CHAPTER TEN
# THE THIRD MAN

"Nothing in a tomb frightens me except another living human. Only a man who draws breath can plot against me, while the actions of the dead are predictable. I knew my way around the traps and dangers of a tomb—I'd been working in them since I was a child. But when I realized that there could be a third man in this chamber, my liver turned into a chunk of ice.

"Who else could have known the undersea tomb was here? Was there someone who had the same information my cousin had received from Jude Kao? It had to be someone who was either on our boat or on one near ours. Had we awoken another person who had then followed us here? Was the third person someone from Wen-Jin's archaeological team? If that were the case, why didn't he let us know he was here and why would he have attacked Jie Lianhuan?

"I needed to bring whoever it was out of cover so I turned off my flashlight, bent down, dropped to the floor, and rolled away from the coffin. Then I went dead still and listened. Other than the thunderous beating of my heart, I could hear someone breathing. Then there was a soft rustling noise as if someone was moving. Shit, I thought, I was right. There is someone else in here with us.

"The minute that thought raced into my mind, all sound stopped as if whoever it was had begun to hold his breath. I began to raise my body from the floor, afraid that the third man might step on me in the dark. Just as I was halfway up I heard the cracking of joints behind me. I tried to move away but a current of air pushed past the side of my face. A gust of strong wind blew out of the darkness and a man hurtled toward me, pushing me back onto the floor. I could feel him tug at my flashlight and pull it free from my belt; then he smashed it into my jaw. My mouth filled with blood.

"God damn it, he can see me, I realized with a jolt of fresh terror. How can this son of a bitch see in the dark? Another blow hit my nose, my head lolled backward, and more blood gushed into my mouth. I choked and gagged, trying to regain my equilibrium.

"Nobody had ever beaten me up before; I had always been the bully, and this attack made me ready to kill my invisible assailant. I pulled out my knife and stabbed at the darkness before me. A heavy punch landed on my chin and sent me to the floor. Then both of my hands were pinned to the ground and I lay there, completely immobile. All I could do was spit and I sent a mouthful of blood toward whoever held me. The man dodged and I twisted my body to escape his grasp. He bent down to pin me with his knees and I knew I had him. As he came down toward me, I smashed at him hard with my sack that held the skull I had planned to give to Wen-Jin.

"I heard a groan and then the noise of someone rushing away. Laughing, I threw my sack in the direction of the groan, then raced over to Jie Lianhuan's flickering flashlight and swept it across the chamber. There was nobody there but I heard splashes in the direction of the spot where my cousin and I had entered. I ran toward the sounds but all that was there were ripples in the water.

"Then I heard it—a horrible hissing sound that made me want to tear out both eardrums. When I turned in the direction of the noise, I almost fainted. The valve on my oxygen tank had been opened and the oxygen was escaping with a steady sibilance.

"When I saw my life span leaking away with the oxygen, my brain almost exploded with fear. Quickly I twisted the valve shut and stood still, unable to move or think.

"My first reaction was rage—at myself. How could I have been so stupid that I failed to guard my lifeline?

"I checked the level of oxygen left in my tank and found only a tenth of it remained. Jie Lianhuan had almost nothing in his—it would be gone by the time he took forty more unconscious breaths. I had used half a tank on my way into this place; I wasn't going to make it back out with what I had now. Was there any way I could save myself?

"I'd have to move five times faster than my entry speed had been in order to get out with the oxygen that I had left. It took us about half an hour to come in; it would be impossible for me to get back out in six minutes. At best, I could manage it in a quarter of an hour. In my favor was the realization that the tides were going out, which would expose the cave's opening to the air on the sea's surface. With luck, I would only need ten minutes' worth of more oxygen than I had—but how would I get that added supply?

"I stared at my reflection in the water that marked my exit—there I was, a man in a diving suit, looking hopeless. Then it came to me. If I took off my diving suit and tied the legs and sleeves together to make a balloon of sorts, I could capture air within that bag. Quickly I tied the sleeves together and filled them with air; then I plunged into the water, untied the sleeves, and took a deep breath. There was my reserve air supply. I breathed for four minutes before depleting it.

"Without a second thought, I stripped Jie Lianhuan of his diving suit and turned it into a second balloon. Filling both suits with air, I felt certain I had my ten minutes' worth of additional oxygen. I grabbed my cousin's oxygen tank, telling myself he was already dead. There was no way I could bring him up with me when he was unconscious, and the oxygen I took from him would buy him no more than a few more minutes of life. At least if I made it to safety, I could send a rescue party back to recover his body. And it was either him or me.

"I put Jie Lianhuan on the coffin platform and found my sack with the broken skull to put under his head like a pillow. Then I dove into the exit tunnel, dragging my improvised air bags behind me. But when I reached the exit, there was no opening, only a coral reef. How did I get off course? I wondered. Quickly I looked at the meter of my oxygen tank; there was no air left in it.

"I couldn't panic. I kicked away my oxygen tank and then connected myself to Jie Lianhuan's. I tried to see where I was but my flashlight couldn't penetrate the darkness that surrounded me. I couldn't even make out where I had come from.

**10. THE THIRD MAN**

"For a second, panic washed over me; then I forced myself to calm down. I still had ten minutes of reserved oxygen in my air sacs. I simply had to find my way out before that time was up—and since my cousin's air supply had just run out, those ten minutes were beginning right now.

"I began to breathe from the first air bag when my flashlight died. But in the pitch dark before me I could see a little green light. It was a light from the dancing corpses—all I needed to do was follow them out of here.

"The figures were drifting much too slowly; the entrance was within sight but by the time I saw it my second air sac was almost empty. With a wild surge of energy, I broke away from the current that carried the cadavers; clumsily I ran into one of the bodies. As I clung to it, trying to regain my equilibrium, I saw a vapor seeping from the corpse that I held. I pressed on it hard. It wasn't a body at all but a hollow figure made out of bamboo—and there was air inside it.

"Grabbing my knife, I stabbed at the shape and gulped at the air bubbles that emerged from it. Pulling two others along with me to supply me with air, I made my way to the surface of the water and then back to my boat.

"By the time I returned, it was already dawn and the sun was about to rise. Once I was safely aboard, I saw diving gear that was still wet in a corner of the deck. There's the guy who tried to kill me, I decided, he's one of us for sure. But when I entered the cabin, everyone there was sound asleep so I pretended to sleep as well.

"A couple of hours later I got up and announced that Jie Lianhuan was missing. We all plunged into the sea to look for him and I was prepared to 'discover' the opening that would take us to the undersea tomb and my cousin's body. But instead Jie Lianhuan's corpse floated in the water nearby. He must have regained consciousness and tried to swim back up without an air supply.

"It was only then that it dawned on me that I had killed Jie Lianhuan. If I'd only gone back for him as soon as I reached the boat and got more oxygen, he would be alive now. This still haunts me as the most despicable thing I've ever done in my life."

As I looked at my uncle's pale and unhappy face, I remembered the message written in blood that we had found near the undersea tomb. Of course Jie Lianhuan thought Uncle Three was the one who had tried to kill him. He'd been knocked unconscious by someone he'd never seen and he had no idea that they'd been followed into the tomb. As far as he knew, he and my uncle were the only people in the coffin chamber, so naturally he thought Uncle Three had assaulted him, taken his diving equipment, and left him for dead.

Still, there was no explanation of how Jie Lianhuan had come across the bronze fish and how his body made it out of the tomb. For a second I thought of telling my uncle what his cousin had written about him before dying, but that seemed unnecessarily cruel.

Uncle Three went on. "I already told you what happened after this when we were in Jinan. Of course, I didn't want you to know that Jie Lianhuan's death had anything to do with me, so I didn't talk about the things that happened the second time I went into the undersea tomb with Wen-Jin and the others. It's true that I was pretending to be asleep after I went in, because I didn't want to take them to the coffin chamber—I didn't know what Jie Lianhuan would have left in there. I was hoping that before they got there, I could check it out by myself. And I knew that the person who had attacked me would eventually give his game away. I wanted to use this opportunity to expose him, so I could take revenge for Jie Lianhuan."

At this point, I thought of the things that Qilin had told me. If I didn't remember wrong, he had made the suggestion to explore the ancient tomb without Uncle Three. A quick burst of suspicion made me ask Uncle Three, "Did you find out who the killer was? Was it Zhang Qilin?"

Uncle Three frowned. "I followed them after they left the chamber. That guy did seem suspicious, but there was someone else whom I found even more disturbing. Anyhow, I think if Qilin wanted to kill me, he would have just broken my neck. He wouldn't have battered me with my flashlight and opened my oxygen valve. Besides, I could never have held my own against him in a fight. I don't think he was the man who attacked me."

I nodded, knowing that was true. "What happened next?" I asked.

"Well then…after Qilin took the group out, I followed. Once they were in the tomb, they went into the chamber with the pool. I didn't know at that time there was a tunnel under the pool, and I thought they'd come out after they looked around. So I waited on the path to the main tomb. But I waited for quite a while and they didn't come back out. I realized something probably had happened to them, so I went in after them. Qilin has probably already told you what happened after that."

"So it's true that you pretended to be a woman in order to guide them through the Strange Doors?"

"What the hell? What do you mean I pretended to be a woman?"

I repeated what Qilin had told me. Uncle Three's eyes widened as he asked, "Say that again."

I went through it one more time and my uncle gasped. "He really said that?"

"That's what I heard."

Uncle Three squinted and made me repeat the story again in detail. I tried hard to remember everything that Qilin had said and meticulously retold his account.

Uncle Three shook his head. "No, that isn't right. He's lying!"

I frowned. "But I don't think he had any reason to lie to me. He didn't even have to mention it."

Uncle Three hit his head lightly, gave the matter some thought, and then said, "You're right. So if what he said was true, there are still many flaws. You see, this kid said 'I' was crouching there when all he saw was the sight of 'my' back. They made up their mind who was there based upon a shadow of a person in a diving suit."

"Ah!" I said. "This makes sense. So it wasn't you, but someone else who had a similar-looking back that led them through the secret trap?"

Uncle Three nodded as his expression became more serious and somber. "If what the young lad said was true, then it's definitely so. Besides, didn't you notice? Qilin couldn't see my face."

I tried to remember everything that Poker-face had

told me, and all of a sudden realized, "Huo Ling! He was blocked by Huo Ling! And she was the only one who said she had seen your face."

Uncle Three nodded. "Right. She was working with the guy who was pretending to be me."

All of a sudden I remembered Qilin saying when he was telling me the story, "If it really was your uncle." Could he also have suspected that the person wasn't Uncle Three?

"But why," I objected, "did Qilin say he saw your face just before he drifted off into that bizarre slumber?"

Uncle Three sighed and said, "That I really don't know. Maybe he mistook someone else for me just as he lost consciousness. After all, he expected my face to be the one he had been chasing. But don't forget: he was in a daze from some kind of soporific drug. It could have been a hallucination."

I shook my head. "I don't agree with that. Qilin wouldn't say he had seen you unless he was positive—that would go against everything he is and does."

"Then he must be lying, because I'm telling you the truth."

Qilin or my uncle—one of them had to be a liar. But their stories did roughly match up, which made me feel less upset. I might not have the whole truth but I was very close to it. However, my uncle's story put a whole new card on the table. Either he was innocent and someone else had assumed his identity, or he had been with the group and was the villain I had feared he might be.

Of the two conflicting stories, I still believed Qilin's account more, because he had nothing to gain by lying to us. On the other hand, Uncle Three's story was very different from the one he'd told me in the past. It was very clear and without any flaws—no lie could have been prepared to such a complex degree. Besides, if he did intend to lie to me, he could have easily done so without having to make up something that was so different from Qilin's story. It seemed as though both Qilin and my uncle were telling the truth.

As I thought of this, a strange idea suddenly came to mind. Since I felt that neither man had lied to me, could there be a situation where both of them were telling the truth?

This was a way of thinking that I'd learned from Fats: all solutions to a problem had to be identified and considered carefully. Even if one possibility seemed to be absurd, it still had to be examined.

I told Uncle Three what I was thinking and he shook his head. "How could that be? If both statements are true, then there had to be two of me in that tomb at the same time."

"Two Uncle Threes." I pondered this for a while. It did seem absolutely impossible. Uncle Three had no twin brother, and he had no body double either. This assumption wasn't logical. However, according to Fats's line of thinking, logic held little importance; all possibilities must be considered—improbable or not.

I took out a piece of paper and started writing down the possibilities. But when I thought about it again, I found that based on the premise that neither of them had lied, there would only be one outcome—that Uncle Three had been outside of the Strange Doors and the man Qilin saw inside was someone who looked like Uncle Three.

**10. THE THIRD MAN**

So the question really wasn't how there were two of Uncle Three, but rather where the person who looked like Uncle Three had come from. There were a few possibilities. One was a stranger who had come up from the sea. Another one was someone who had been hiding in the tomb all along. Neither of these ideas was very convincing. So the third possibility would be that it was someone from the ten individuals present at that time.

This idea had some credibility. But who could it be? I had never heard Uncle Three mention that anyone in the team looked like him. Now that the subject had been brought up, he would have certainly remembered a person who resembled him if there really was one. Could someone have made himself up to look like my uncle, the way Poker-face had when he pretended to be Baldy? Impossible, I realized, disguising one's looks would take three to four days of preparation and at least five to six hours of makeup. Who had that kind of time in the undersea tomb?

I grimaced as I reached another dead end, and my uncle asked me what I was thinking. I told him and he laughed. "That's what you get for following Fats—his brain is way too convoluted for any normal person to make sense of." Then he turned serious. "Holy shit, could this actually be the answer? Now that you analyzed it this way, I think I understand what's really going on…but, if this is true, then this whole thing is completely crazy. You said that there might be someone among the group that looked a lot like me in the ancient tomb. This makes sense. But I think that this person probably didn't have to look a lot like me. Think about it. Qilin was drugged by whatever created that sweet scent in the room, so naturally he was disoriented. And the fact that he fell into a coma a few seconds later proves that the person would only have to look just a little like me for him to make that mistake."

I nodded. "That's true. But who could that have been? If there was such a person on your team, you would have noticed it. After all, it's very unusual for two people in this world to look alike."

Uncle Three had a befuddled expression on his face. Then he took a deep breath, shook his head, and said, "You're wrong. In fact, there are many cases in the world where it's not surprising for two people to look a lot alike. And on the archaeological team that year, there was a person who looked 70 percent like me, yet no one was at all surprised."

"Impossible." I exclaimed, "Who?"

Uncle Three looked me straight in the eye and replied, "Jie Lianhuan."

## CHAPTER ELEVEN

# THE MAN WHO WASN'T DEAD

I stared at my uncle, thinking he must have lost his mind. He looked back at me calmly as though he had just told me what he wanted to have for dinner. Pulling myself together, I managed to ask, "How could that be possible? He was already dead."

"Indeed. He was certainly dead; his body was swollen and in a state of rigor mortis when it was found. But then please remember, the boat that took his body back to dry land vanished. It was never proven that the body we found in the sea was really my cousin," my uncle announced. "You know, I sometimes think I underestimated Jie Lianhuan."

"What do you mean? You think he faked his death?"

Uncle Three nodded. "If he hadn't died, everything we've just discussed has a rational explanation."

"But you were certain that he had died," I sputtered. "There must be another explanation."

Uncle Three sighed. "Let's just drop the whole thing for now. Without Qilin to add his insights, we'll only go around in circles. Once we find that young man, we can analyze everything from the very beginning and maybe this will make sense.

"So, moving on," my uncle continued, "Jude Kao's team was

blown to blazes when we set fire to the tunnel at the cavern of the blood zombies. We met after that and agreed to cooperate in an expedition to the undersea tomb. That fell apart, and Ning came away with only photos of the murals. Then we all set off for the palace in the clouds and you know how that turned out."

It was only much later that I came to know how much information my uncle kept from me as he breezed through the end of his story. At this point I was so horrified by his theory about Jie Lianhuan that it was all I could think about. My uncle went off to the bathroom, leaving me alone with my thoughts.

For Uncle Three, the experience in the undersea tomb was the beginning of a nightmare. It was also the turning point of his gradual change from a small-time bandit to an obsessed man who invested his entire lifetime in order to find the archaeological team that disappeared in the ancient tomb. He had sacrificed all he had—money, time, and success—in his search for the woman he loved.

And now here he was, old, ready for retirement, and with a nephew hounding him for answers. He'd lied to me in an attempt to keep me out of the mess he was in, and it hadn't worked.

The most important piece of information my uncle had just given me was this: when he and Jie Lianhuan left the boat, they were followed by a third man who somehow knew about the undersea tomb and planned to kill them once they reached it. And that person was part of Wen-Jin's expedition.

Of the ten members of the group, excluding Uncle Three, Wen-Jin, Qilin, Huo Ling, Jie Lianhuan, and the guy who took the corpse back to land and disappeared before getting there, there were four people left. And one of those four was a woman, so that narrowed the suspects down to three. Was one of those men the person who impersonated Uncle Three, as well as the man who tried to kill him and Jie Lianhuan?

Then there was Jude Kao—what did he want? First his goal was to decipher the silk book, then it broadened to include the cavern of the blood zombies, the undersea tomb, and the palace in the clouds. Why? He was ninety years old and near the end of his life—his aim couldn't be more money or fame. What was it?

When Uncle Three returned to the room, I told him what I'd been thinking. "Yes," he nodded, "I've thought the same thing and what I came up with was Jude Kao wanted to explore all the places where Wang Canghai had been, as though he were following in that great man's footsteps. I think he was looking for something that Wang Canghai might have left behind."

"Something left in the ancient tombs?" I asked. "Could it have been the bronze fish with their encoded secrets?"

"I'm not sure," he replied. "And you know, I don't care about what the hell he wanted. I only want to find out what happened to Wen-Jin and the others. I watched Jude Kao because the Xisha disaster was somehow related to what he was doing, but it all became so damned complicated. I decided to beat him in discovering whatever he wanted to find, so I could blackmail the old devil into telling me the truth about Wen-Jin's fate. But unfortunately I'm getting old and my strength doesn't match my ambitions anymore."

I patted him on the back. "We came to the end of this adventure when we reached the palace in the clouds. Ning and her team failed in their goal of getting inside the coffin there so they'll probably try it again. But that's the last stop. Whether they find what they're looking for or not, this is where the journey ends. Stop being so stubborn, Uncle Three; you've done your best but we're finished."

My uncle's smile was grim. "The end? It seems like it's too soon to say." He picked up the videotapes Qilin had sent, tapped them lightly, and said, "This is definitely not the end. Let's see what's in here before we come to any conclusions."

My uncle had sent his assistant out hours ago in search of a VCR and he still hadn't come back. It wasn't an easy quest; everyone had switched to DVDs, and again I wondered why Qilin had chosen to send us such an outdated medium. As I thought about what might be on the videotapes, I felt a stab of fear. Uncle Three was old and tired and I was in no way capable of carrying on his search for him. I had hoped the adventure had come to a close but Qilin's package was about to reveal new twists and discoveries. I almost hoped that we wouldn't be able to view the tapes, as cowardly as that was.

We knew nothing about Zhang Qilin, aka Poker-face. We didn't even know whether he'd joined Wen-Jin's expedition by chance or if he had an ulterior motive. He'd never given any of us, not even my uncle, a scrap of personal information. It was impossible to guess what he might have put on these damned tapes. When Uncle Three's assistant came back saying the markets had closed before he could go to them all and he would have to resume his search the next day, I was glad for the temporary reprieve.

I was so happy that I sneaked Uncle Three out of the hospital for some real food and a bottle of wine. With a cigarette in one hand and a glass of wine in the other, my uncle announced he was ready to discharge himself from the hospital and told me to book him a room at a nearby hotel.

He went off with his assistant to settle up with the hospital. I found a hotel with adjoining suites, took a hot bath, and felt immeasurably better. As I waited for Uncle Three, I took out my laptop and opened the file with the old photograph of Wen-Jin and her team before they went to sea.

I had looked at this picture so many times. Uncle Three looked dignified and reserved in the photo; you'd never guess he was a grave robber. Qilin looked like a typical student. I tried to look for Jie Lianhuan and found a person who looked quite a bit like Uncle Three. That had to be him. Who would ever think there'd be so many secrets hidden in such an ordinary photograph?

Then I got onto the website of the express courier that Poker-face had used to send his package, typed in the tracking number, and searched for the shipping information.

Soon the results came up. I pulled the cursor down to the column of the mailing address. It wasn't blank. There was a city's name—Golmud: this was where the videotapes came from.

I froze for a moment. Where was this place? I looked it up immediately and felt even more surprised. It turned out to be a city in the western part of Qinghai Province, not too far from Tibet.

Qinghai? When did Poker-face go there? I became suspicious. This guy really moved around quickly—in a matter of days he'd left the mountains and gone to the west. He might have gone to offer his expertise to the grave robbers of that region—but it wasn't a spot where our line of business was practiced.

I looked up some information about Golmud and was even more baffled. It was a city that had been built long ago by the

People's Liberation Army, surrounded by the Gobi Desert. I really couldn't think of what Qilin would be doing there, and why he sent me two videotapes from that place. All of a sudden, I wanted nothing more than to watch those damned videos.

The next morning a call from Uncle Three's assistant woke me. "Your uncle is next door and wants you to come over. I found a VCR early this morning."

Uncle Three sat smoking in silence when I entered his room. The VCR was ready to go so I inserted one of the tapes, shuddering a little as I did it. There was a bit of static at first and then an image appeared.

It was a room in an old wooden house; it held a very old-fashioned desk with a file cabinet, a small lamp, and a phone that looked as though it dated back to the end of the twentieth century. Impatiently Uncle Three pressed the fast-forward button. All of a sudden, a black shadow flashed across the room.

Uncle Three quickly rewound the tape and played it again in slow motion. The shadow turned out to be a woman wearing a ponytail. She looked quite pretty and was walking very fast; she passed across the screen in a flash and then disappeared.

Uncle Three lunged forward, his face almost touching the TV screen.

"What's wrong?" I asked but he waved at me as he growled, "Shut up."

A few minutes later the woman reappeared, having changed into pajamas; she walked straight in front of the screen, which began to shake. Apparently she was adjusting the angle of the camera.

**11. THE MAN WHO WASN'T DEAD**

This was equivalent to a close-up. The woman's face was directly in the middle of the TV screen. I could see that she was young and very cute. Her eyes were big and her face looked sweet and kind.

Uncle Three began to tremble. He pointed at the woman's face as he shouted, "Huo Ling! It's Huo Ling!"

All I knew about Huo Ling was that she was the child of party officials and had been one of Wen-Jin's group of students. That she was in this video was completely bizarre; and it also seemed eerie that she knew she was being filmed. What the hell was going on here?

Why did she want to make a video like this? How did this tape get in the hands of Qilin and why did he send it to me?

As we watched, the woman sat down near the desk, picked up a mirror, released her ponytail, and began to comb her long hair. She tied it back up into a ponytail again, stared out the window, and ran from the room. When she returned, she had changed her clothes again.

Once again she adjusted the camera and her face again filled the entire screen. I heard my uncle moan, as though her pale countenance frightened him. Then she sat back down near the desk, untied her ponytail, picked up the mirror, and began to comb her hair again. Her combing motions and their frequency were almost exactly the same as before; again she tied up her hair, stood up, and trotted out of the camera's range.

She came back with another outfit on and began to adjust the camera angle one more time. Then she stopped. I looked up and saw that Uncle Three had hit the pause button so the screen was filled with a close-up of Huo Ling's face.

My uncle had no color in his own face, and his hands

were trembling. He peered closely at the face on the screen and muttered, "Damn it all, she didn't get any older either! Qilin stayed the same over the years and now so has this girl. God damn it, how did they all stay young, all of them who disappeared? What the hell happened to them?"

"Calm down," I told him. "We don't know when this video was filmed, do we? Or how old Huo Ling was when this was taped. Don't get hysterical."

Uncle Three pressed play and the video continued, but soon there was only static. We waited but no image reappeared; Uncle Three fast-forwarded to the end of the tape; it was all static. "What's wrong?" my uncle yelled, pounding his hand against the VCR.

I stopped him, took out the tape, and examined it closely. "It's been erased." I said.

Uncle Three and I stared at each other. The tape had to have been erased before it was sent. But if it had been done intentionally, then why leave anything in the beginning? Could there be something at the end that we weren't meant to see? What was Qilin trying to tell us?

Uncle Three put the tape back into the VCR and rewound it in hopes of finding something we didn't see the first time. After all, we had fast-forwarded the first section—who knows what we might have missed.

This time we watched the whole thing second by second. Not a sound was heard in the room. We stared until our eyes were bloodshot but we saw nothing that could be a clue.

Then we played the other tape, but it was entirely blank. Everything was static. We rewound it and watched the static twice, finally turning off the VCR when we began to feel dizzy, confused, and thoroughly frustrated.

## 11. THE MAN WHO WASN'T DEAD

Uncle Three was in no mood to talk after we turned off the VCR. We sat thinking for hours and found no comfort in our confused thoughts. At least we had learned that the missing archaeological team hadn't died in the undersea tomb decades earlier—or one of them hadn't. Huo Ling had survived up into the 1990s, although she seemed a little unbalanced, to say the least.

I forced myself to watch the tapes a few more times but still saw nothing useful. Huo Ling's behavior never seemed anything other than insane to me. My uncle made copies of the tapes and gave the originals to me. Then Panzi showed up and took my uncle and his assistant back home to Hangzhou.

"Leave this matter alone, Nephew," Uncle Three told me before he left. "If anything new turns up, tell me at once. You've been lucky so far but your luck has almost run out in the grave-robbing world. Go back to selling books and antiques; someday you'll inherit my business too, if I haven't lost everything in my crazy quest by the time I die."

"Don't worry," I promised, "I've had more than enough adventure—the quiet life seems good to me at this point."

Before I returned to Hangzhou, I made arrangements to have dinner with some old college friends who lived in Jilin. As we caught up on what we had done since our student days, I told them a little bit about my recent activities. None of them believed me so I pulled out the photograph of my uncle and the archaeological crew before they set off on their expedition.

"These are the people who were the catalysts for my adventure," I insisted. "Of the ten on this team, eight disappeared without a trace."

One of my friends took me seriously enough to say, "You should go to the National Archives, and check out which archaeological team with eleven members disappeared twenty years ago. Then you might actually get somewhere."

"You mean ten members," I corrected him.

"No, I mean exactly what I said—eleven. There are ten people in your photo, but who was taking the picture of the group?"

"You're right," I said slowly, "why the hell didn't I think of that?"

Back when that photo was taken there were no point-and-shoot cameras, and there would have been no photo studios in that tiny fishing village in Hainan. In those days, the fishermen there would have had no idea of how to handle a camera—the person who took the picture had to have been one of the archaeological team.

But in Uncle Three's account of the story, he had always referred to ten people—never eleven. Could the photographer have stayed behind and not gone out to sea or was my uncle hiding something from me again?

Seeing my face become serious, my classmate said, "No need to worry over this. There were few archaeological groups at that time—just go to the Archaeological Institute and look for the files on this team. You know how our bureaucracy works—those office files never get thrown out. You'll find all the information you need with no trouble at all."

I knew it wasn't that easy. If I found out there had been eleven people in the group that Wen-Jin led to the undersea tomb, then what? I'd be right back on the trail again, this time without my uncle, who would have been proven a liar. I was finished with this, I told myself. It was time for me to become a solid citizen with a placid life again.

## 11. THE MAN WHO WASN'T DEAD

## CHAPTER TWELVE
# AN UNEXPECTED GUEST

My return to Hangzhou would have been peaceful, if it weren't for Fats. He came to town often, spending money like a madman as he scooped up antiques for his newly opened shop in Beijing. I always knew when he was approaching my store because I could hear his voice booming outside; this afternoon he came in swearing and furious.

"Two vases," he fumed. "I brought them with me on the train to sell here, packed them myself, and the damned idiots still managed to break them. Of course the railway refuses to compensate me for destroying my baggage—what's a comrade to do, Young Wu?"

"If you weren't such a cheapskate, you would have flown here, Fats. The vases would have been carry-on luggage and now you'd be able to sell them both for enough to pay for your airfare fifty times over. It's your fault for being so miserly."

"What would you know about making money? It's a waste of time to talk to you—it's your uncle who knows how to fill my pockets. What's he up to now, anyway?"

"Uncle Three and I have been taking a little break from each other right now. He's still worn out from his latest caper; I don't think he has anything planned in the way of the family business. He may have retired from all that nonsense. I know I sure as hell have."

Fats rolled his eyes skeptically. "Sure. Right. Let me know when that old fox is ready to prowl through some dirt again."

"All you ever want is money and more money, Fats. Won't you ever have enough?"

"Someday you'll learn—once you have money, it's only human nature to want more. If you ever get any for yourself, you'll find that's true."

As I laughed, someone burst into my shop, calling out, "Oh please—tell me you're open."

Before I could see who it was, Fats had erupted with "Shit, what are you doing here, you little hussy?"

It was Ning.

She swept past Fats, ignoring him, smiled at me sweetly, and said, "What a quaint little place you have here. It's really charming."

"Such a surprise to see you," I replied. "Now what do you want?"

Her smile faded as she said, "You're certainly blunt so I will be too. I came to see if you would take me out to dinner, since I don't know anyone else in this city. Will you please?"

For such a small, pretty girl, Ning could certainly pack away the food. She was silent as she devoured every scrap on the table. She wiped her mouth carefully with her napkin and observed, "Hangzhou food would be good if it weren't so sweet."

Fats snorted. He hadn't wanted to come with us but I

tempted him beyond his limits; a free meal was all it took to persuade him to spend time with Ning. Neither he nor I ate very much. I didn't trust Ning enough to be able to relax with her and I was quite sure Fats didn't either. She had something up her sleeve—I just hoped it wasn't a poison dart or two.

"I had no idea you were such a connoisseur of fine food. You were eating more like a starving prisoner than a gourmet critic of China's regional cuisines," Fats taunted. He glanced at me as though he wanted me to join in his sarcasm but all I wanted was to get to the heart of this meeting.

"So I fed you dinner, and one that I'm sure you could have bought on your own. Tell me now, why are you here?"

Ning smiled. "Why so suspicious, Young Master Wu? Can't I just come to see you because I enjoy your company?"

For some reason, my chest tightened and my face turned hot. I was sure I was blushing. Fats turned his head away and said nothing, which was both a relief and an embarrassment. Ning continued to smile at me before she replied, "I've never known what you're thinking, but I'm sure right now you're just pretending to be bashful. I guess I should try being serious. You're right. I had a reason for finding you." She took a box from her handbag. "Our company just received this in the mail. Take a look; it's something that involves you."

As I held the box in my hands, I knew what it was. I sat stunned; it was Fats who grabbed the box and tore it open. Inside were two black videotapes.

**12. AN UNEXPECTED GUEST**

"These were sent to our headquarters in Shanghai a few days ago. Because the sender was rather unusual, they were quickly transferred into my hands," Ning said. "After I saw the contents, I knew I had to come and pay you a visit."

"What's so unusual about the sender? What's on the tapes?" I asked.

Ning glanced at Fats and with a faint smile on her face, she turned to me again and said, "The sender is very unusual. The sender of this express delivery—"She took an express company's receipt from her bag. "See for yourself who it is."

I took the paper from her hand as Fats leaned over to peer over my shoulder. The name of the sender turned out to be my own.

"You?" Fats bellowed.

I quickly shook my head and said to Ning, "I didn't send this; it wasn't from me."

Ning nodded. "We knew that. Why would you send us anything? The person who used your name apparently did this to make sure the package would be given to me."

"What's on the tapes?" Fats interrupted.

"It's quite strange. I thought you guys should watch it and see for yourselves."

"Is there a woman on it who keeps combing her hair?" I blurted.

Ning was clearly a bit puzzled by my question. She glanced at me and shook her head. "No. What's on these—well, I don't even know if you could call this normal human behavior."

Fats. Ning, and I went back to my shop and I sent my

clerk to my house to get the VCR we'd bought in Jilin. In the back room of the shop we connected it to a small TV and turned on the tape.

Like the ones I had received, this one was filmed in an old wooden house. But the layout wasn't the same as the one we'd seen in Jilin—this room was much bigger. It was dark with only a little light coming through the windows; the furniture was different and there was nobody there. The picture remained the same for fifteen minutes. Then Ning made a quick gesture with one hand and Fats and I leaned closer to the screen, knowing something was about to happen.

A gray shadow emerged, moving in from the darkness. Its movements were very strange and slow, as if the person was drunk. Soon the shadow became clear, and when it finally moved to the side of the window, we realized why its movements were so peculiar. It wasn't walking; it was crawling across the floor.

We couldn't tell if it was male or female. It was wearing the kind of garments that are put on a dead body before burial; it looked as though it had been dressed quickly and carelessly. It moved like a person who was disabled or had been terribly injured—very slowly and with great difficulty.

Once on the news I had seen footage of a woman who was mentally ill and whose husband had locked her in a cellar for years. When she was finally released, she could no longer walk upright, but could only move in a squatting position. The creature on this videotape reminded me of that woman.

We watched it for almost ten minutes and its silent,

painful crawl was difficult to witness. Then it crawled out of the range of the camera and disappeared. Ning turned off the tape. "We don't have to watch anymore—that was the important part right there."

"What the hell is this all about?" Fats asked.

"What do you guys think you saw?"

"Why do you even ask? Isn't it a person in a house crawling on the floor?" Fats replied.

Ning ignored him, looked at me calculatingly, and asked, "What about you?" It was as if she thought I might have seen something different.

"Isn't that what you saw?"

Looking a little puzzled, she squinted her eyes and asked, "You...didn't recognize anyone as you watched?"

Baffled, I shook my head.

Ning stared at me for a long time, sighed, and said, "Well then, we'll go to the second tape. I hope you're ready for this." She put the second tape into the VCR and skipped through the first fifteen minutes. Then she looked at me and said, "You...take a deep breath."

I was feeling a trace of panic, but Fats was getting pissed off. "Don't condescend to this guy—don't you know who you're talking to? He's seen it all, from the crest of snowy mountains to the bottom of the angry sea. I don't believe you have anything that could scare him in this tape. Don't project your own feminine fears on him. Tell her, Young Wu—there's nothing she could throw at you that would disturb *you*—am I right?"

I ignored him and told Ning to start the tape. She glared at Fats and the video began to play again. The scene was still within the same room, but the camera lens seemed to be shaking a little, as if someone was adjusting its position. After quivering for a bit, the lens became still and a face emerged from the bottom of the screen.

The camera was unfocused at first so the image wasn't very clear, but I could tell the face didn't belong to Huo Ling or any other woman. Then the person shifted backward a little; he was wearing a gray burial suit, sitting on the floor, trembling. As he turned toward us, I could finally see him clearly.

Fats let out a yell as he looked at me and I felt as though I were choking. The face on the screen looked insane but it was very familiar. It belonged to me.

## CHAPTER THIRTEEN
# ABSOLUTE MADNESS

The three of us sat for at least ten minutes, Fats staring at me the whole time, but nobody said a word.

Ning had paused the video. On the black-and-white screen, the freeze-frame showed a face that I looked at every day when I brushed my teeth. For the first time in my life I felt such indescribable terror that I wanted nothing more than to take to my bed and never get out of it again.

Ning finally broke our silence. "That's why I had to come and see you."

I didn't answer her; I didn't know what to say.

Fats opened his mouth and uttered a few sounds that weren't words before he finally managed to spit out, "Young Wu, is that you?"

I shook my head and felt a gust of vertigo wash over me. My mind was blank. I squeezed my temples with both hands and hoped Fats and Ning would stop asking questions and give me some time to calm down.

They left me in peace while I took a few deep breaths and forced myself not to vomit. Then I asked Ning, "Where was it sent from?"

"The receipt says it was sent from Golmud in Qinghai."

I took another deep breath. Sure enough, both packages were sent from the same city. The tapes we just watched were of the same vintage as the two that featured Huo Ling, sometime in the '90s. These two tapes and the ones I received were definitely related. But I knew I had never worn clothes like that, nor had I ever crawled across the floor of an old house. This was way too bizarre—that person on the screen wasn't me.

"Besides this, did you receive any other clues?" I asked Ning. She shook her head and replied, "The only clue is you. That's why I came to find you."

I picked up the remote control in a white-knuckled grip, rewound the tape, and watched it again. During the close-up, I had to force myself to look; the person on the screen had my face, beyond a doubt.

Fats began to ask more questions but Ning stopped him. She called my shop clerk, gave him some money, and sent him out into the cold. He returned with a bottle of wine and Ning poured me a glass.

Gratefully I drank a huge swig, and then began to choke a little. In a gentle voice I'd never heard come from him before, Fats said, "Calm down; don't hurry. This isn't hard to explain. First, are you sure this isn't you?"

I shook my head and replied, "This man definitely isn't me."

"Then do you have any brothers that look a lot like you?" Fats grinned suddenly and asked, "This question came up before and you nearly took my head off. Are you sure your father had no—oh, you know…"

Again I shook my head and gulped down some more wine.

**13. ABSOLUTE MADNESS**

Ning stared at me for a long time and then said, "If it wasn't you, then can you explain what this is about?"

"How the hell am I supposed to know?" I shouted. The whole thing was completely beyond my understanding or any sort of rational thought. But at the same time, something was teasing my brain, some sort of weird awareness that I couldn't grasp.

"If it wasn't you," Fats said, "this person might be wearing a mask that looks like you. It seems like this person is obsessed with your looks, which ought to make you feel good—he thinks you're handsome, obviously. Do you suppose someone shot this video to play a trick on you for some reason?"

I cursed silently. A mask made to look like me, perhaps made of human skin, was actually a good explanation, but it still left a lot of questions. Who wore it? How did he know what I look like? What did he do while wearing my "face"? Why did it appear in a video? Where was the place in the video? When was this filmed? How was this connected to Huo Ling's tape?

"It's not that simple, Fats. There has to be some deeper reason why these tapes were made and why my name and Zhang Qilin's were written on the packages as the senders. But I can't think right now."

I went off to bed, retreating into sleep, trying not to dream. Ning went back to her hotel and Fats found a room near my shop, saying he wasn't going to leave until we had this mess straightened out.

The next evening the two of us went out to eat and Fats leaned across the table. "Young Wu, now that woman isn't around, can you tell me what the hell is going on?"

"I really don't know. It's not because of Ning that I'm acting muddleheaded."

Fats looked unconvinced. From his point of view, my Uncle Three was a huge liar, so I would naturally be the same kind of person. In his mind, the person in the video was absolutely me, and there had to be some sort of indescribable trouble that kept me from telling him the truth. When the food was served, he took a sip of wine and asked me again, "Young Wu, this whole thing is horribly complicated. You haven't said a word to me all day. Have you come up with any sort of explanation for your being in that video? If you have, don't you dare hide it from me."

I frowned and said, "I really haven't thought at all; I don't even know where to start. The only thing on my mind now is who in the hell sent those tapes. But I do realize that Huo Ling and 'I' both knew we were being filmed and obviously 'I' didn't care. Huo Ling's tape was obviously made around the '90s. If both sets of tapes were shot around the same time, then the 'me' in Ning's tape would also be from the end of the century. But I was still a teenager. I was in high school then—I looked nothing like the adult 'me' on that tape. But how would someone in the '90s know what I would look like as an adult? It's all so crazy, Fats. Who made this? If he's trying to scare me to death, he almost succeeded."

Fats patted my shoulder. "Could the person who sent this tape to Ning be Zhang Qilin pretending to be you?" I sighed. Who knew? If the person who sent the package to Ning used my name, then could the person who sent me the tapes be using Qilin's? But if it wasn't Qilin, then who could it be? Could it be someone in the Xisha expedition? And what was the purpose behind all this?

"Oh, Fats. You think differently from other people. Help me out on this one. Judging from your intuition, what do you think this whole thing is about?"

"Intuition?" Fats scratched his head and said, "I have no background in this mess. How could I have an intuition?"

That's true, I thought. It was a bit ridiculous of me to ask Fats that. After all, he wasn't that close to Qilin, and he didn't know much about Xisha, or at least not as much as my uncle had just told me.

Come to think of it, what did I know about Zhang Qilin? My gut feeling was that he wasn't quite human. Other than the few times that he had saved my life, I couldn't remember him doing anything more than sleeping. I didn't even have the slightest clue of how to describe his personality. He didn't have any distinguishing habits, he never did anything more than what was necessary, but the minute he made a move, something would happen. And on the rare moments that his expression changed from his usual poker face, everyone around him started to feel very nervous.

I thought a bit more and said to Fats, "Forget about intuition then. Why don't you talk about how you feel about this whole thing? What don't you think is right? Even a little bit of your opinion is fine. Show me some support."

Fats sighed and said to me, "God damn it. You're really a disgrace to the proletariat. I don't have any feelings about this, but I did notice something, a little detail when you were talking just now. Didn't you say that there were two tapes that Qilin sent you, one of them with a woman combing her hair, and the other one blank?"

I nodded. Fats said, "That's what's fucking wrong about it. If it's blank, why did he send it to you? Why didn't he just send one? "

"I thought about that in the beginning, but because the whole thing was so fucking bizarre, I didn't have much energy to brood over this one small illogical detail. I only thought that there had to be a reason but I didn't know what it might be."

"We live in the real world. This isn't a movie—something so illogical doesn't just happen. I think we might have complicated this a bit too much. Maybe the person who sent the tapes had a very simple reason for doing it."

"What do you mean, Fats?"

"It's not really an idea. I just think you're looking at this from the wrong angle. Think about it more directly. The person sent you two videotapes, one with something on it, the other one blank. That means he didn't have to send one of them at all, but he sent it anyway. Am I right?"

I nodded and Fats went on. "Because the person who sent the tapes seems so mysterious, we believe that everything he did carries some profound meaning. But damn it, suppose whoever sent this stuff was just a normal guy—do you think under normal circumstances an ordinary person would do something like this? I don't think so—if I were to send you a tape, why the hell would I include a blank one in the package? Wouldn't that be crazy? There's got to be some hidden reason here. Am I right?"

**13. ABSOLUTE MADNESS**

I nodded. Fats always surprised me with the depth of his thoughts. Leaning back in my chair, I considered his question.

Under what circumstances would an ordinary man mail one videotape with something on it and one that was blank?

Don't complicate this, I told myself. And then when I thought about the past, my heart stopped for a second. Once when I was young, I did the same thing.

Fats looked at me. "What is it? What did you think of?"

"Shut up for a minute," I hissed at him. As I mulled this over, more memories rushed to the surface. Jumping to my feet, I yelled, "Holy fuck. It's that simple! Stop eating. We've got to get back to the shop right now."

Fats almost choked on a mouthful of food. "Stop eating? I didn't even have any lunch today. What kind of a host are you anyway?"

"Fine—then join me when you've finished eating, okay? I'm leaving now without you."

Fats got out of his chair, shouting at our waiter, "Don't take this food away—I'll be back and if I find one slice of onion missing, I'll take it out of your hide!" Then he followed me out the door.

CHAPTER FOURTEEN

# THE SECRET OF THE VIDEOTAPES

The restaurant wasn't far from my shop. I raced back, found the two tapes, grabbed a screwdriver, and began to unroll one of the tapes from its case. If I was right, then this whole thing was really very simple.

One of the two tapes turned out to be blank. That indicated the tape with contents wasn't important. The sender wanted me to get the tapes, not what was on them—and there could be only one reason why this package was important. I unspooled all of the tape and carefully shook the case. Sure enough, there was some paper sticking to the inside of the plastic container.

"Fucking hell, how did you think of that?" Fats asked.

I grinned. "You thought of it." I pulled out the paper. It was a page from a memo pad with a few words scribbled on it: No. 349-5 Deershen Lane, Kunlun Road, Golmud, Qinghai Province.

This was ingenious. For one thing, the case kept the address from being torn or crumpled while it was in transit. Also, if the package had been intercepted, whoever took it probably wouldn't think something would be hidden this way, especially when what was on one of the tapes was so enigmatic.

It was clear to me that the sender wanted to keep this address from Uncle Three, who had been completely distracted by what was on the first tape.

I removed the tape from the other case. Instead of a piece of paper, it held an old brass key, the kind that was popular in the 1980s. It was so old that it had turned black. A bit of adhesive tape had been stuck behind the top of the key; under it was a scrap of paper bearing the number: 306.

"Looks like whoever sent this is inviting you to come for a visit," Fats said. "Even got you a room."

Looking at the address and the key, I sat dumbfounded. Fats was right. Evidently the person who sent these videotapes really wanted me to find the key and the address and then go to that particular house. It seemed as though my host might not be at home when I arrived. Did he want me to break and enter?

Suddenly I had the strangest idea. This might be Qilin's house; could he have known somehow that he might not come back through the bronze doors? Had he instructed someone to send me his house key as an inheritance?

If so, I might be able to find out more about his past if I went to his home. But that was unlikely…besides, there might be something else hidden in the two tapes that Ning had shown me.

I rarely had a cigarette, only when I was particularly upset, but I chain-smoked my way through the entire night as I sorted through thoughts that only brought confusion. Discovering the real purpose of the videotapes just gave me more headaches. Why were these particular videos chosen to conceal the address and the key? And who were the people chosen to impersonate Huo Ling and me?

Tonight Fats made me wonder if I had made this more complicated and murky than it was ever meant to be. Maybe the whole thing was quite simple and the answers to all of my questions were right in plain sight.

Of course I was most concerned about the tapes sent to Ning that were supposedly of me. Up until now, I felt uninvolved in Uncle Three's quest, just tagging along for the hell of it. Now I was part of this mystery too, but I couldn't think of one thing that could possibly connect me to it, other than being Uncle Three's nephew. I certainly had never crawled on the floor of a dark house, dressed in clothing meant for the dead.

As I thought my way through the long night, I remembered something my college friend had told me when we had dinner in Jilin: "The reason why this has become so complicated is because you're always depending on getting answers from your uncle, but you aren't sure that he's telling you everything. If you really want to find out what's going on, why not look for the answers yourself? You could do the research to find out whether there were ten or eleven people on that expedition. It's a much better way to learn the truth than going crazy wondering whether your Uncle Three is lying or not."

He was right. Damn it, if this had something to do with me, I really couldn't trust anybody. I'm not going to involve anyone else this time, I decided. I'll go to Golmud alone and take a look at what this is all about.

14. THE SECRET OF THE VIDEOTAPES

## CHAPTER FIFTEEN

# THE HOUSE OF MOLD AND MILDEW

Two days later I was on a plane to Golmud, a city close to Tibet and high in the mountains. Almost immediately after I got off the plane, the altitude hit me and I passed out before I even left the airport. I came to on the floor, lurched to my feet, and found a counter that sold a remedy for altitude sickness. Washing it down with some Tibetan butter tea from a nearby street stall, I managed to make my way to a hotel, left my bags in my room, and then rushed out to hail a taxi.

When I showed the driver the address that I'd found in the videotape, he shook his head. "Can't get you there," he said, "it's an old neighborhood and the roads are too narrow for a car. I can drop you off nearby—it's the best I can do."

As we made our way to the old part of Golmud, I saw that the houses in the area were ramshackle wooden structures dating back to the '70s. I felt as though I was on the right track and set off into the twilight, feeling optimistic. The streets were almost deserted and I roamed through them aimlessly, finding no signs or house numbers to guide me in my search.

Just as I was ready to give up, a pedicab pulled up and

offered me a lift. I climbed in gratefully, and felt even more fortunate when I found the driver spoke my dialect and had lived in Golmud for twelve years. He looked disappointed when I turned down his offer to set me up with a girl for the night but brightened when I showed him the address I was looking for. "Yes, I know where that is. It's not too far—I'll take you there."

He took me to a road that was so secluded I was afraid he was going to rob me and leave me for dead. Instead he stopped in front of a dark three-story building and smiled. "Here you are. It used to be the People's Liberation Army's Nursing Home but it's been abandoned and empty for years."

There was a faded house number on the gate of the place and when I peered at it through the darkness, I saw it was the one I was looking for. It looked haunted in the fading light and I turned back to the driver. "Who lives here now? Is there a caretaker?"

"I have no idea," he replied. "All I know is it was built in the 1960s when there were a lot of soldiers here. After that, it was a theater for a while, and I used to go to movies there. That's why I knew where it was." He waved goodbye and drove off, leaving me alone on the street. One streetlamp nearby provided the only illumination. I felt a little apprehensive and then laughed. I'd been in tombs that were much more threatening than this—what was my problem?

I pushed at the gate; it was locked. But the streetlight was close to the walls that enclosed this place. I was able to climb up and then jump down into a yard filled with weeds. There was a house with old wooden windows, all gaping open. I climbed through one of them into an empty hallway that was covered with a thick layer of dust.

Luckily I had brought a pack of cigarettes with me so of course I had a lighter. I struck a flame and saw that I was standing in the hallway where "I" had crawled across the floor in the videotape.

I've come to the right place, I thought. The floor and the carved windows were exactly what I'd seen in the tape. Fear and excitement washed over me as I walked deeper into the house toward a spiral staircase. I took the key from the videotape out of my pocket and looked at it—306. I needed to go to the third floor.

As I glanced at the stairs ahead, I saw footsteps in the dust. Someone had been here before me, and not too long ago. I tested the first step cautiously; it creaked but bore my weight. I started to climb.

On the second floor there was a cement wall that lay beyond the staircase; I continued my ascent without stopping. On the third floor was a long, dark corridor with rooms on either side. The hallway was draped in cobwebs and smelled stale and musty. Numbered doorways stretched to my left and right; the second to the last was 306. The key fit in the lock and the door swung open easily.

Slowly I stuck my head into the room, gagging at the reek of mold and mildew. The streetlight that had allowed me entry shone through a window and I could see there was nobody inside waiting for me. I took a deep breath and walked in.

It had been someone's bedroom. A small bed in the corner was covered with a rotting quilt, and a desk stood nearby. Beside the desk was a cupboard as tall as I was and at least thirteen feet wide; it was badly water damaged. I looked at the ceiling above and saw large stains where the rain had soaked through.

Why had I been sent to this place? What was there for me to find in this hideous little room? I put my lighter on the desk and began to rummage through the drawers. Nothing. What about the bed? I walked to it and looked underneath. Nothing. I pulled out a desk drawer and used it to poke at the quilt to see if it concealed something. All that I saw under the filthy cloth was a puddle of black liquid filled with bugs; I gagged and turned away.

Now only the cupboard was left to ransack, but its door was locked and I had no tools to open it. I looked around for something I could use to force the lock open or to break down the door.

The window had an old-fashioned lock with a bolt that could be pulled all the way out. It was metal, solid, and very sturdy. Using it as a tiny crowbar, I inserted it into a crack in the cupboard door and pulled hard until there was a space large enough for my arm to get through. I reached inside and yanked at the door with all of my strength. Slowly the wood gave way and snapped, releasing a blinding cloud of dust. When I could see again, I picked up my lighter and thrust it into the cabinet, feeling sure there would be nothing there.

And I was right—except there was a gaping hole in the back of the cupboard, revealing a hole in the wall behind it, an open trapdoor that was half as tall as I was. It led to a cement stairway going downward.

Looking at the key in my hand, I knew that it had been

given to me so I would find this trapdoor. The answer I wanted was at the bottom of the stairs and I had no choice but to walk down them. I stepped through the door and immediately a strange smell filled my nostrils.

The stairway twisted and I couldn't see the bottom. Fear began to get the upper hand but I reminded myself I was in a city, not a tomb site. I began my descent.

I had only gone a few steps before a frigidness swept toward me from the bottom of the stairs; suddenly I could see my breath puff out in little clouds. I shivered as I continued to walk down. On either side were cement walls covered with military slogans painted in red. Wires hung from the top of the stairs, swaddled in spiderwebs that made them look like snakes.

The stairs continued far below what should have been the first floor of the house—is there a basement, I wondered, or perhaps even a military bunker under this place? Shuddering from the increasing drop in temperature, I went down another flight of stairs. It ended with a doorway that opened into a large room that was nothing more than a simple concrete basement, damp, cold, and empty.

I walked toward the center of the room where something cast a huge horizontal shadow on the floor. I walked toward it, holding my lighter. In the middle of the basement was a huge, black coffin that looked as ancient as any I had ever seen before.

**15. THE HOUSE OF MOLD AND MILDEW**

## CHAPTER SIXTEEN
# TRACES OF HUO LING

Why would there be a coffin under a military nursing home? And who was in it? Could it be an officer who died here back in the day? But it definitely wasn't modern—it was carved from black stone in a style that was used more than half a millennium ago—and it was so mammoth that it had to hold someone important.

I walked over and touched it. It was carved with a small pattern that was obscured by the layers of dust. Raising my lighter high, I saw chisel marks on the coffin lid and a crack where a crowbar had been inserted to pry it open. Someone had been here before me.

How did an ancient coffin get into the cellar of a twentieth-century building? What magic could have brought it here? My mind was in more turmoil than I could handle right now. Each time I thought I was approaching some answers, I only uncovered more unsolvable questions.

I tugged at the lid of the coffin and was relieved to find I couldn't open it. I needed companions with me as well as tools—I really didn't want to face this alone. I walked around the coffin to the other end of the basement. There was a small iron door; I pushed it open and found another corridor.

I had only taken a few steps before I realized the structure here was exactly the same as on the third floor. There was one corridor with rooms on both sides. The only thing different was that this corridor seemed as though it went on forever. There were no doors to the rooms; they lay open on either side of the long hallway.

Walking into the first room, I saw two desks placed side by side against the wall. There were some file cabinets, and papers were scattered everywhere on the desks and the floor.

This seemed to be an office. Things were getting increasingly bizarre. Why would there be an office underground? Baffled, I walked over to the closest desk in hopes of finding a clue. As I came closer, I suddenly stood stock-still. I didn't know why, but the placement of the desk gave me a chill in my belly. I'd seen this room before. It was the room where Huo Ling had been in the videotape.

The desk, the floor, the wall were all exactly the same. I walked to the side of the desk and even saw the mirror which she held when she combed her hair. It was still in the same spot that it had been in the video.

When I saw Huo Ling in the video, I thought she was in somebody's house, not in the basement of a nursing home. But I was here, looking at where she had been filmed. Obviously everything was true. The contents of the tapes were real.

Huo Ling had really filmed herself with a video camera here, as she repeatedly combed her hair—and "I"—"I" could have very possibly crawled across the lobby above the spot where I was standing now.

16. TRACES OF HUO LING

For a moment, I even saw Huo Ling before me as though my world and hers had suddenly overlapped, and scenes in the video flashed before my eyes.

But what on earth happened here? A woman secretly hidden in the basement of a nursing home who kept combing her hair; someone who looked like me crawling across the floor of this nursing home's lobby looking like someone who had been crippled—all these things truly happened and had been recorded on videotape. But why? What had been going on here beyond the range of the camera?

My brain turned numb and I began to feel dizzy. Clearly the purpose of the person who sent me the videotapes was to lead me to this room, but I now had even more questions than before. I felt as though I was solving a puzzle with no clues, with no place for me to start putting it all together.

Once again I took several deep breaths and calmed myself down. Then, I raised my lighter high to study this place and see what clues I could find here.

In this hidden basement of this mysterious nursing home lived a bizarre woman whose behavior bordered on madness. Certainly she must have left some trace of her presence behind her. If I could find anything to prove she had been here, perhaps I could piece together why she had been in this place.

I began to search, scrutinizing everything I could see, beginning with the walls nearby. There was a rod for hanging clothes and a large, empty cupboard, which was perhaps where Huo Ling had made her costume changes. An opening in the wall led to the room next door, which was completely empty.

Next I examined the two desks. The papers on them were trivial things like electric bills and lists of random numbers—perhaps old phone numbers. In a drawer were some dust-covered notebooks. Flipping one open I saw three lines on a page:

Backroom: 2-3.
Number: 0.12-053
Category: 20, 939, 45

I turned the page and there was a picture—a badly drawn sketch of a fox with a gigantic mouth and a human body. Lines were drawn around it, and after staring, I realized they were meant to represent a landscape around a temple.

Turning the next thirty or forty pages, all I found was the same drawing. Was this more evidence of Huo Ling's madness? In the next notebook, I found the same thing. Besides these, all that was in the drawer was a bundle of cloth. If there had been any useful information, it was all gone now.

But I was unwilling to give up. I didn't believe everything could have been taken away without one small trace left behind. I sat down where Huo Ling combed her hair and pulled at the largest desk drawer. It was locked but its heaviness told me there was something inside.

I pulled one of the rods out of the wall and pried at the drawer. I pulled hard and it opened. "Yes!" I shouted to the empty darkness. The drawer was full of things that had plainly belonged to a woman—a comb, a powder compact, hairpins, and movie magazines dated from the 1990s, along with unused envelopes, all of them empty, and a photo album with all of its pictures removed.

So Huo Ling had been here—or some woman who looked like her—but I still had no idea why. I shivered with cold and frustration—there had to be a clue somewhere that would tell me what had been going on. I got up to examine the second desk.

The middle drawer in this one was also locked so I used my trusty clothes pole and broke into it. There was a manila envelope, bulging with something inside. I grabbed it and pulled out another old notebook; this one contained writing in clear and legible penmanship that looked familiar. Greedily, I began to read what it said:

I don't know which one of you three is reading this, but whoever you are, you probably already have become involved in this by the time you find this letter. We sent the videotapes as our last hopes of getting assistance. Once they are mailed, whoever receives them won't be able to contact me. I'll either be dead, or *It* will have found me, and I will have left this city. In either case, this means that I may soon leave this world, so I hope the videotapes will guide you to this place and lead you to my notebook.

It's the record of over ten years of research and experiences. I will leave it for you guys; in it you'll find the things you're trying to learn about.

However, I must warn you that its contents involve a dreadful secret. I once vowed to take it to the grave with me, but in the end, I can't keep my promise. After you read about this secret, your fortunes will hang in the balance and you will have to be very careful.

Chen Wen-Jin
September, 1995

## CHAPTER SEVENTEEN
# WEN-JIN'S JOURNAL

Wen-Jin—I remembered her careful handwriting from the notebook I had found in the undersea tomb. Was she the one who sent me the videotapes that brought me here? I had thought of her as being dead for so long—it was shocking to have her reappear. Why had she brought me to this place and why had she brought me more damned questions? Which three people was this addressed to? What was "*It*"? Who were "we"? What research? What secret? Countless thoughts flashed across my mind and I didn't have time to ponder any of them. Pulling myself together, I turned the pages of the notebook and began to read.

The book began with a precise and delicate little drawing of only seven strokes—six curved lines and an irregular circle. It was the pattern from the silk book that Uncle Three had sketched for me not too long ago. How did Wen-Jin know about this?

However, the difference from Uncle Three's drawing was that this one had a black dot on each of the six curved lines. Next to four of these dots, I could see some tiny printed words:

Changbai Mountain----Cloud-Top Palace of Heaven
Temple of Seeds----Seven Stars Lu Palace
Reclining Buddha Ridge----Sky View Temple's Pagoda
Shatou Reef----Undersea Tomb

As I carefully studied the curved lines, I realized they formed an image of a dragon—head, tail, and its four limbs much like the pattern Chen Ah-si had pointed out to me in my uncle's tea shop a few months ago. Each line represented a mountain range, and each black dot was the treasure site on that range. This pattern didn't represent only an ancient map of the stars—either Jude Kao was completely wrong or he had lied to Uncle Three.

Next, I looked at the two lines without any words written next to them. They also had dots and were each labeled with a question mark. Obviously this was also part of the dragon, but the locations of these sites were unclear. Then I noticed that beyond the six curved lines was another black dot, all by itself. And beside it was Wen-Jin's tidy printing: "Tamu-Tuo." Underscoring this name were several very deep lines drawn with a few more question marks next to them. Obviously this was the most important dot on the map.

Tamu-Tuo? Could this also be the site of an ancient tomb? Why was this dot outside of the lines? I flipped further ahead in the notebook and found both text and pictures. As I read, I felt more and more puzzled and deeply disappointed. When I finished reading, I sat motionless, wooden and confused.

The notebook was a work log written in the form of a diary that consisted of three separate parts.

The first part read as follows:

April 2, 1990
We numbered most of the porcelain in the undersea tomb,
sketched almost all of the pieces, and compared them with
the murals in hopes of finding out about the life of Wang
Canghai. Through this comparison, we found a number
of regular patterns. The murals depicted the experiences
of his life, and the paintings on the porcelain documented
his construction projects, except for the final mural,
which broke that pattern. This showed a nobleman saying
goodbye to someone, with a huge palace in the background.
The palace was very grand, but appeared on none of the
porcelain pieces, which we thought was peculiar. A place
this sumptuous should have had a corresponding porcelain
painting.

Later as we studied Wang Canghai's life, we discovered his
final years were draped in mystery. There was no historical
data left behind, as though the end of his life was completely
blank. Why? This became an overriding question for us.

December 6, 1990
We have been investigating the whereabouts of Wang
Canghai in the last years of his life, and finally we found
a clue. We discovered that after he completed his last
known project, he went with the emperor to the Changbai
Mountains on a ceremony of worship. From then on he kept
no more written records.

December 7, 1990
We changed our research to concentrate on the emperor,
where we found records of diplomatic missions and grand
ceremonies. We found that seven grand ceremonies took
place in the two years before the emperor's death. Six of
the ceremonies were normal, but one was very strange. The
record was very simple without any marginal notes:

"Forty-six guards, twelve soldiers, a hundred and twenty-six
horses, ten decaliters of pearls, thirty catties of gold, and the
envoy sent to Tamu-Tuo."

A grand ceremony and a mission—this might be what we
were looking for, but who was the envoy and where is Tamu-
Tuo? Is it a country? There's no official historical record,
but this is very plausible. There were many small kingdoms
in Southeast Asia and the Western Territories during the
Ming dynasty. This could be one of them. But it seemed a
bit bizarre that Wang Canghai would serve as an envoy to a
small country. Why would a man of his age be sent on such
a long and difficult journey?

February 11, 1991
The investigation continues. We compared the things that
were brought on the Tamu-Tuo mission and found from the
type of gifts that this was probably a country in the Western
Territories. The number of gifts seemed very few. However,
there were many horses, which suggested that it might be a
trade caravan rather than a team of ambassadors.

## March 6, 1991

We have found no clues, no breakthrough. Our research has stalled and nobody is in a good mood.

The next section jumped ahead two years.

## January 19, 1993

It looks like Wang Canhai's journey to Tamu-Tuo was connected somehow to the emperor's ceremonial visit to the Changbai Mountains. He had probably returned to the Cloud-Top Palace of Heaven, and then left for Tamu-Tuo. This Tamu-Tuo mission must have had something to do with the situation in the Changbai Mountains.

## April 18, 1993

We decided to head for the Changbai Mountains and check out our theory. The weather is terrible; we've lost contact with the rest and the two of us are moving on alone.

## June 17, 1993

We reached the palace and the situation is horrendous. The others are probably dead. We don't have time to hesitate; we're going to go through the bronze doors and see what lies beyond.

## June 18, 1993

My God, what have we done? I have seen the Ultimate!

**February 8, 1995**
We are planning to find Tamu-Tuo. I must find out what all this is about.

"I have seen the Ultimate!" I felt sick as I read this. What did Wen-Jin mean? Why did she write nothing else for over a year? She was so meticulous that this seemed completely out of character. Had she, like Wang Canghai before her, seen something beyond the bronze doors that was too shocking to comprehend or describe?

My strongest feeling was that Tamu-Tuo had a huge connection with the bronze doors. It was only after Wen-Jin had gone through that portal that the idea of looking for "Tamu-Tuo" dominated her attention.

Then came the third portion of the notebook:

**February 10, 1995**

Based on the map of the Dragon Path, we have confirmed the location of Tamu-Tuo. We will conduct an exploration and hope to find the answer to a series of puzzles. To be honest, I really didn't think there would be so much behind all this. If what I saw behind the bronze doors was indeed real, then this whole thing is unbelievably horrifying.

She then described the journey to Tamu-Tuo, which seemed to be an oasis in the Gobi Desert. In early 1995, Wen-Jin launched an expedition to the depths of the Qaidam Basin.

They were led into the Gobi Desert by a female guide named Dingzhu-Zhuoma. Then on a rocky hill they parted ways, and alone the group entered the place called Tamu-Tuo. The journey from then on sounded very dangerous and many died along the way. There were also notes on the road map that marked numerous signs of trouble. They finally reached Tamu-Tuo, where Wen-Jin had an argument with one of her group. In the end, she came back without making any significant discoveries.

I scanned through this part very quickly. There were many details that I skipped over, road maps, descriptions of equipment failure, and accounts of bad weather. What I wanted wasn't there.

There was nothing about their investigation or how they came across the information in the journal. It mentioned nothing about the disappearance in Xisha or anything about this nursing home. What concerned me most was that there were clearly missing portions between the three parts, which made me think the journal had been bound by someone other than Wen-Jin, or else it was a copy of her original notebook.

But when I tried to find a trace of rebinding or torn pages, I saw this was the complete journal. In other words, this was a notebook copied by Wen-Jin. She seemed to have included only the contents about Tamu-Tuo in this record.

Why did she do this? Why did this group of people have to be so secretive? Could there be something in the rest of the journal that she didn't want others to know about?

As I read through this notebook, I had a very clear feeling that she was trying to tell me that Tamu-Tuo was very important. It was as if she wanted to lead me there.

I rubbed my temples, flipped the notebook back to the first page, and prepared to carefully read it from the beginning one more time, hammer away at it again, and see if I could find some answers. But the fuel in my lighter was running low and soon I'd be in the dark. Thinking I could make a little bonfire out of the wood from the desk drawer, I stood up and stretched.

And then I knew something was wrong. I raised my lighter; there was a shape sitting on the other side of the desk, looking into the mirror and combing its hair.

## CHAPTER EIGHTEEN

# DARKNESS

The shape was peculiar with a neck so long that it was almost giraffe-like. I was sure it was a woman, calmly and slowly combing her hair. She terrified me.

Who was this person? When did she appear, sitting on the chair, looking into Huo Ling's mirror and combing her hair...could this "person" be Huo Ling?

I took five to six steps backward, stopped, pulled myself together, and asked, "Who are you?"

I hadn't spoken at all since I entered the basement, and now that I asked this question, my voice sounded hoarse and strange to my ears. In this silent room, my croaking speech still came across loud and clear; yet the other person didn't respond to my question. No words came back to me from behind the desk. It was as if I were talking to empty air.

God damn it, I cursed to myself, are you trying to scare me? You're doing a fine job. Considering the weird shape of this body—could this thing be inhuman? But that was impossible. That would only occur in an ancient tomb. This is a modern building; there couldn't be anything like that here. It's not like there are any coffins...wait, hold on a second. That's not right! Fuck. There is a coffin here!

Could this be a zombie from the coffin?

At this moment, a thought flashed across my mind. Was this person the one who sent me the videotapes? Could she have been waiting for me here?

After reading the notebook, I thought the person who sent the tapes was Wen-Jin, but I couldn't be sure. She could have told someone else to send them to me and then meet me here after I arrived.

It seemed plausible. This basement wasn't a place that an ordinary person would know about. Someone who could find their way here had to be an insider. The sender of the tapes could have been waiting for me in the vicinity and then had emerged at the right time after I came in. This thought put my mind at ease, so I gathered up my courage and told myself there was no need to be afraid if this were a living person. I stretched out my arm that held the lighter to see who on earth it was.

I carefully walked a few steps closer. The "person" sitting there had disappeared.

I squinted in the dark light; the person was gone. Was it my imagination that it had been there at all? No. I had seen it, I was certain of that. I swooped my lighter higher into the air and fanned it in all directions, but my motion was too abrupt. The lighter went out and I stood in pitch blackness.

I shook the lighter and tried to reignite it but only managed quick flashes of flame that lasted for half a second at a time. It was out of fluid.

Cursing to myself, I stepped back in the direction of the staircase and heard a soft noise that sounded like a woman's laughter.

Then I felt a chilly sensation on my neck. The ceiling of the basement was very low; I could touch it just by raising my arm. Although I couldn't see anything, I involuntarily looked up. In the darkness I felt a fluffy mass of something touch my face. I grabbed at it—it was wet, stringy hair and lots of it.

Ever since coming back from the undersea tomb I hated the feeling of wet hair, and now my throat closed up as though I had swallowed a rat. Quickly I ducked and swung my head to shake off the wet strands that were trying to cover my face.

Grabbing one of the strands, I sniffed at it and smelled an unpleasant and familiar odor. I couldn't remember at first where I had smelled it before, but I knew it hadn't been a good experience. Then I heard that whisper of laughter again, coming from the ceiling. I immediately took a few steps back and crashed into the desk. The impact sounded like thunder in the quiet basement and frightened me even more.

I stood up, shivering like a wet dog, and the sound disappeared. Then I felt a tickle on the back of my neck. Holding my lighter tightly in one hand, I found the flint and moved it as hard as I could. A spark ignited the last drip of fluid and in that flare of light I saw a huge swath of hair hanging from the ceiling. From its center a grim, white face stared at me.

I knew who it was. I'd seen this before. As the light went out, the face still was clearly imprinted on my mind—it was the Forbidden Lady from the undersea tomb, or one of her relatives.

I panicked. Shrieking and turning around, I bolted backward and ran straight into the darkness. I only had one thought in mind: I had to escape from this place.

I didn't get very far before my whole body smashed into the wall with suicidal power. I fell to the ground, and when I crawled to my feet, I could hear noises from overhead coming straight at me. Blood filled my throat but I didn't care. I groped for the opening that had been my entryway to this hellhole. Stretching my arms in front of me, I found my way out and raced into the corridor, slamming the door shut behind me. I moved along, searching for the staircase, but in the darkness this wasn't easy.

Then I tripped over something and sprawled full-length. "Oh, shit," I groaned. I had landed on the coffin. I touched it, fumbling, and realized it was different. Its lid had been pushed open. How did this happen? But I had no time to think; rising to my feet again I continued to try to find the stairs.

Then I heard something move close by; a hand came out of the blackness and clapped over my mouth. An arm encircled my body, immobilizing me, and a man whispered harshly, "Don't move."

I knew better than to struggle. I knew that voice. It belonged to Zhang Qilin.

YOUNG MASTER WU

## CHAPTER NINETEEN
# REUNION

The minute I heard his voice, my body turned numb and my mind went blank. As far as I knew, Qilin could be anywhere in the world, or even nowhere in this world. But there was absolutely no reason for him to be here. Slowly questions flooded my brain like tidewater—why would he be here, what was he doing here, had he sent the videotapes, was he hiding here, was he, like me, only here to investigate? I thought of him walking through the bronze doorway and I wanted to grab him by the throat and choke an explanation from him.

But he had me in a vise grip. I couldn't move and he wasn't loosening his grasp. All I could do was listen—to a loud squeaking noise at the door. Something was forcing it open. I held my breath and strained to hear what was coming for us. There was a strange popping sound and then silence. All sounds stopped, the hand fell from my mouth, and a match flared in the darkness.

There was Qilin, the same as always. I stared at him, speechless, as he walked to the door and closed it. Then he raised the match toward the ceiling, staring up at it. I opened my mouth to speak and he gestured for me to remain silent.

I, too, looked at the ceiling—there was no hair, no face, no Forbidden Lady. How could she have gotten to this place? What the hell was going on?

Qilin looked around in a circle very thoroughly. After confirming there was nothing hiding, he came back to where I stood.

"Didn't follow you out," he said softly, staring at the door.

All of my questions almost exploded out of my mouth, but he spoke first, asking casually as though we'd seen each other only the day before, "What brings you here?"

I felt the blood throb in my temples and all I wanted to do was jump on him and choke the breath from his body. What the fuck? I thought. Asking me a question when I have so many for you? Does this look like a place where I would want to come? If it weren't for those videotapes, I never would have shown up here!

I gritted my teeth, wanting to launch into a tirade, but as I stared at that impassive face, I found myself reluctant to let loose as easily as Fats often did. I clamped my jaw tight for a long time before I answered, "It's a long story…Why are you here? Where on earth is this place? You…didn't you walk into the bronze doors as I thought you did? What the hell is going on?"

These questions were really badly put, but I had to ask them, even if they emerged in a confused jumble.

"As you said, long story." He turned away from me, his attention absorbed by the black coffin. I looked over and found that the lid had indeed been pushed open, but it was dark inside. I had no idea what might be lying within it.

This was what I hated about this guy. Whenever I asked any key questions, he was always like this. But before I could open my mouth to repeat my interrogation, Qilin told me to be quiet. Then he lowered his head and looked inside the coffin.

Under the light of his match, I could see that the coffin was empty. It was clean, as if nothing had ever been there, but there was a hole at the bottom, and a small sound came from it. After a second or two, a hand stretched from the hole, and a man crawled out from the narrow opening like a cockroach from a drainpipe. Then he emerged from the coffin and stepped beside us.

I gaped like a kid at a magic show as the man wiped the sweat from his forehead, looked at Qilin, waved something in his hand, and whispered, "Got it."

Qilin seemed to be waiting to hear this; he gave my shoulder a push and muttered, "Let's go!"

I followed the two of them, carefully making my way along the same route that had brought me in. We'd gone only a few steps back up the stairway when we heard the door in the corridor behind us squeak loudly as it opened.

The stranger leading the way cursed and then started to run. I immediately followed behind, and we ran all the way out. It wasn't until we jumped over the walls in the yard that I breathed a sigh of relief.

I leaned against the streetlight, panting and completely out of breath, but the two didn't stop. After they jumped over the walls, they continued to run, without looking to see whether I was with them or not. I'm not going to let you get away this time, I thought, and chased after them.

We ran all the way out of the old part of the city. Suddenly a car loomed ahead in the dark, the door opened, and the two men rushed over and jumped in. Just as the door was just about to close, someone held it open long enough for me to leap inside too.

I was gasping for breath. Once I got in the car, I felt paralyzed. I closed my eyes and took a few deep breaths before I finally calmed down.

I looked around and once again I was dumbfounded. The car was filled with people, all of them looking at me with polite smiles. The most surprising thing was that I recognized a few familiar faces. They were part of Ning's team from the palace of doom. Seeing my shocked expression, several of them began to laugh and one of the foreigners said in broken Chinese, "It must be destiny that we meet again though we were thousands of miles apart." Then I saw Ning's head sticking out from behind one of the seats, looking at me with an astonished look on her face.

I looked at Qilin and then at the person who crawled out from the sarcophagus just now, a young guy wearing sunglasses. Neither of them was out of breath at all and both were staring back at me. Drowning in confusion, I asked, "You bunch of morons. Who can tell me what the hell this is all about?"

Ning replied, "That's my question for you. How come you were in that basement?"

"You first," I told her.

As the car raced out of the city of Golmud and sped into the Gobi Desert, Ning told me what had brought her to this place. It turned out that she too had found the same address and key inside the videotapes she received. Apparently she was one of the "three people" mentioned in Wen-Jin's journal. After she discovered the secret, she immediately made a two-part plan of action. First she sent some people to look for this address, and then she came to see me in person in Hangzhou to find if I knew anything about the contents of the videotapes.

But she didn't know that I had also received videotapes, and had discovered what she had found. We all reached the nursing home at almost the same time.

Thank goodness I moved fast, I told myself, or they would have found Wen-Jin's journal, not I. Touching the notebook in my pocket, I was glad I had accomplished so much the first time I acted on my own. My discovery wasn't part of the story I told Ning; this was my secret.

"How did you and Qilin join forces?" I asked.

Ning smiled. "Your uncle isn't the only one who can afford to hire that guy. He and his pal named their price and now they work for me as my consultants."

"Consultants?" When Ning mentioned the word, I immediately remembered Fats appearing on the search for the undersea tomb. Ning's a fast learner, I thought. This time she hired a reliable source of knowledge. But it felt really strange that Qilin would work for Ning. I felt a bit betrayed.

"Don't listen to her nonsense," one of the foreigners broke in. "She's not the one who hired these guys—she's just an employee herself. Your pals answer only to our boss, and they are the real heads of this expedition. They make all the major decisions and we provide technical support. Our boss said we need to leave the professional work to professionals from now on."

It must have been the high death toll at the palace of doom that had caused this change. "So what's this all about—what was on the videotapes, what's up with the appearance of the Forbidden Lady? Do you guys have any idea?"

Everybody's gaze turned toward Qilin and his new friend.

Ning glared at them and muttered, "We don't know any more than you do. We're just following them, and as you already know, they aren't the most informative people in the world."

Before I could ask anything else, the car stopped and the driver shouted, "Grab your bags, everyone. We're here."

We got out to find a dozen Land Rovers parked in the wasteland of the Gobi Desert. Gear was piled in mountains on the sand, and bonfires illuminated the night sky. A huge satellite dish stood nearby and a crowd of people bustled about. All the vehicles were the same shade of white and all bore the same name—Acropora.

As we emerged from the car, people began to cheer. "What's going on?" I asked again.

One of the foreigners grinned at me. "My friend, we're off to Tamu-Tuo."

I stared at him. I'd never heard of this place until I read the name in Wen-Jin's notebook, which these people hadn't yet seen. How did they know about it?

"What's going on?" the guy asked. "You just turned pale."

"Nothing. Just a little exhausted. What do you mean by Tamu-Tuo? What are you going to do there?"

"Tamu-Tuo?" The guy glanced at Ning, who was walking in front of us. "I'll tell you about it later. Let's go and check out what your friends have brought back with them."

The campsite was enormous. Ning led us to the largest of the many tents and we crowded inside. A Tibetan guy poured us all some tea and I looked at the group that surrounded me. Most of them I didn't know and when I looked at Qilin for some sort of clue as to how to behave, he pissed me off by closing his eyes and relapsing into his customary meditation.

His friend in sunglasses handed something to Ning and she

put it on a low table where we all could see it.

It was a flat mahogany box. She opened it, and there was a blue and white porcelain plate with a piece broken from one side. What was so important about this?

Two Tibetan women entered the tent, one middle-aged and the other quite old. Everybody except Qilin and his friend turned toward them as they came in, and several people bowed their heads toward the old lady. She returned the courtesy and stared at me, probably because I was the only person she had not yet met. Ning picked up the porcelain plate, handed it to her, and asked, "Lady Ma. Please look at this. Have you ever seen this before?"

The middle-aged woman repeated this in Tibetan and the old lady took the porcelain plate, examined it, and began to nod. She poured out a torrent of words in her native language, so fast that I couldn't keep up with the translation. My old pal Wu Laosi was beside me and I asked him, "Who is this woman who's speaking?"

The guy with sunglasses leaned toward me before Wu Laosi could speak. "Her name is Dingzhu-Zhuoma. She was Wen-Jin's guide."

I nodded politely while my mind continued to whirl. Not only did this group know about Tamu-Tuo, they also had found the guide. They probably even knew what had become of Wen-Jin.

I found out about Wen-Jin's expedition, leaving from Dunhuang and moving through Qaidam's hinterland, only because of Wen-Jin's notebook—and she had mentioned hiring a female Tibetan guide. But in the notebook Wen-Jin had said that once they had passed Qaidam and entered the Chaerhan Region, the female guide couldn't find her way anymore. In fact, there was no longer a path to follow. The guide left the group and they set off on their own to who knows where. It seemed as though this old lady would be little help in taking this new expedition to Tamu-Tuo—at best she could only guide them to the spot where she and Wen-Jin's team had parted company.

As I was lost in my thoughts, the two Tibetan women left the tent and people burst out with questions. Ning smiled as she replied, "She said this was the plate that Chen Wen-Jin had shown her long ago. She is willing to guide us to the mountain pass where she and Wen-Jin went their separate ways. We're on the right track."

"When do we leave?" the guy with sunglasses asked.

Ning stood up. "Today at noon. Everyone will go." People began to leave the tent as Qilin's friend asked, "What about him?" and he jerked his chin in my direction.

Ning pointed at Qilin and laughed. "He's the one making the decisions. Ask him." She led the others out of the tent, leaving me with the poker-faced mute and his mysterious friend.

The guy in sunglasses lit a cigarette and leaned toward Qilin. "You're the one who let him in the car. If we'd left him behind, we'd be spared the trouble of his presence now—what are you going to do with him?"

Qilin opened his eyes and stared at me. He sighed and spoke at last. "Go back. There's nothing here that concerns you. And don't return to that nursing home—what's in that place is way too dangerous."

To be honest, I didn't even want to go with them—I just wanted to clear up this mess of confusion in my skull. "Sure, I'll go. But first I want you to answer my questions."

Qilin shook his head. "You'd never understand if I told you. Besides, I'm still looking for answers myself." Then he stood up and walked out of the tent without uttering another word.

This put me in a killing rage. I'd never hated anyone as much as I did this dismissive, condescending son of a bitch. The guy in sunglasses saw the fury in my eyes and smiled. "We'll send you back to the city, don't worry about anything. Happy trails." He followed Qilin, leaving me alone in the tent.

Now my rage became complete humiliation. I'd been tossed aside like a used piece of toilet paper. But I had been sent the tapes, perhaps by Wen-Jin herself. I was part of this, whether Qilin liked it or not. There was no turning back for me. Even though part of me wanted to go home and forget everything, at this point that was completely impossible. I had to go on this journey, no matter what. After all, I was the one with the notebook in my pocket. And I was my grandfather's descendant—I couldn't dishonor him by abandoning the search that might possibly clear his name.

I went outside and found Ning, who was packing up her gear. "I need some equipment," I announced. "I'm coming too."

"Stop joking with me. I don't have time for this," she sniffed.

"It's no joke. You know you can use me—remember what happened at the palace of doom."

She turned back to look at me and her face changed. "Are you serious about this?"

I nodded, and she pointed to a pile of gear. "Take what you need and make it fast. We're leaving at noon and we won't wait for you if you aren't ready. We have quite a journey before we reach Tamu-Tuo—and some of us may not make it there alive."

## CHAPTER TWENTY
# INTO THE DESERT

As our fleet of vehicles sped through the desert, they stayed far apart to avoid eating each other's dust. Ning gave me a brief rundown on the route we'd be following: first to Dunhuang, then to Qaidam and on to Chaerhan. There we'd leave the highway and drive into the no-mans-land of the Qaidam Basin, with Dingzhu-Zhuoma leading the way to the place where she had parted with the expedition long ago. This was almost exactly the same path that Wen-Jin had described in her notebook. How in the hell did Ning get this information? She knew about Tamu-Tuo, Dingzhu-Zhuoma, and this route, almost as though she had read the notebook that I had carefully tucked away from prying eyes.

The desert that we raced through gave me an eerie feeling of having been abandoned in its unending stretch of sand. Nothing lived here—no people, animals, or vegetation of any kind. The loneliness of it was suffocating and I was grateful when we stopped to make camp, forming our own little village.

I sat beside a German guy named Hans, a chatty, outgoing sort who happily answered my questions. The information he provided made me realize that I was making things overly complicated again. It wasn't necessary to have read Wen-Jin's notebook to know the things that Ning did. She had found out in the most direct way possible—by asking the express courier company who had really sent the videotapes to her. It turned out to have been Dingzhu-Zhuoma, who provided the rest of the information.

"It's strange," Hans told me, "Wen-Jin told her guide that although Tamu-Tuo was reputedly the spot where Wang Canghai had ended his travels, nobody knew what he did there. She was determined to go there to find out why. Before leaving on their journey the Lady Ma found out this place was the legendary Empire of the Queen of the West, a spot otherwise known as Taer Musiduo, the Haunted City of the Rains. She was afraid to set foot in this place, so she lied to Wen-Jin that she couldn't find the way there. Then she left the group to live or die on their own.

"The Empire of the Queen of the West—isn't that just a myth?"

"Not at all," Hans said. "It truly existed as an ancient country with a very long history. But over time its history became legend and the queen became a divinity to those who heard about her. As Dingzhu-Zhuoma was told, this city only appears during a heavy rain, and if ever you laid eyes upon it, your eyes would be wrenched from your head, leaving you stone-blind. That was why she was afraid to go there."

"So you mean to say that what we're looking for right now is the ancient capital of the Empire of the Queen of the West?"

"Yes," Hans continued. "If Tamu-Tuo was really in the Qaidam Basin, it had to be part of the Empire of the Queen of the West. Even though we said we're off to find Tamu-

Tuo, we're really trying to find traces of the empire. There's something there that this expedition has been sent to find."

As I remembered, the Queen of the West hadn't been anyone to mess around with—could her empire have been Wang Canghai's final diplomatic mission? And why?

"By the way," Hans interrupted my thoughts, "I see that nobody gave you the clothing you need to survive the desert." He threw a bag to me and told me to change my clothes. As I dressed, I noticed a familiar number, the one that had provided the code to open the puzzle lock—02200059.

"What's this number for?" I asked Hans when I rejoined him after putting on my new outfit.

"Our boss likes to use that—I've heard it came from one of the ancient silk books he had found in his travels."

So my encounter with some of the facts, true to form, provided me with another unanswered question.

Soon we left the highway and Dingzhu-Zhuoma began to lead the way. She was always accompanied by her grandson Tashi and the middle-aged woman, who turned out to be her daughter-in-law; the three of them rode in the car at the front of the fleet with Ning. Our route became more and more difficult, studded with rocks, and we all grumbled over the discomfort of our travels.

At the end of the first day, we reached a small village, which is where, the Lady Ma told us, she and Wen-Jin bought horses and camels for their journey into the mountain pass. We were lucky to have gotten that far, because one of our vehicles turned out to have a cracked axle and was no longer drivable. Not only did we have to leave it behind, we also had to leave the crew and equipment that it had carried, which was a big blow. A pity we didn't have camels instead, I thought; so much for modern progress in this ancient part of the world. How many more vehicles would we lose to this unforgiving terrain?

I kept these thoughts to myself, but Tashi felt the same way and wasn't afraid to say so. "People die in the Qaidam Basin every year and have since the beginning of time. You people are mad to think your vehicles are going to survive this part of the world and if they don't, neither will you. You think today was rough going—wait for tomorrow—and the next day will be worse than that. Even if you reach your goal, you will still need to drive around aimlessly in search of who knows what. Don't underestimate the dangers you face."

"What advice do you have for us?" Ning asked.

"Prepare for the worst."

Hans snorted contemptuously and in a low voice told me, "This boy is a troublemaker. He never wanted his grandmother to make this trip—he says that to do this for money is a sin and will bring danger upon us all. He only agreed to come with us out of respect for the Lady Ma, who is determined to take us to the very end. But if he can discourage us from continuing, he will. The only thing to do is ignore everything that comes out of his mouth."

The desert after dark was cold, the wind piercing. We all had trouble sleeping that night; the sound of low voices from our tents went on for hours. A bonfire provided warmth and light which I found comforting and I stayed awake, watching the flames, long after the voices went silent. I fell asleep, but jerked awake as I heard footsteps close by. I sat up, instantly alert, and saw Tashi standing before me.

Before I could say anything, he squatted down and clapped his hand over my mouth. "Don't say a word. Get up and follow me; my grandmother wants to talk to you."

## CHAPTER TWENTY-ONE
# WEN-JIN'S MESSAGE

Why did Dingzhu-Zhuoma want to see me? I had never spoken to the old lady before; I'd laid eyes on her perhaps three times—why had she sent for me in the middle of the night?

Tashi saw my confusion. "Please come with me. It's very important."

I rose to my feet, he immediately turned around, and we walked away from the bonfire into the desert darkness.

Dingzhu-Zhuoma and her daughter-in-law were both seated on thick blankets that were spread on the ground near their campfire. With them was somebody else—my good old silent partner, Qilin.

The firelight's flicker showed me that Dingzhu-Zhuoma's face was twisted into a grin that looked malicious—could she be upset with me? Why? We had never spoken to each other.

Tashi gestured for me to sit down and the daughter-in-law brought me a cup of tea. I thanked her as I glanced over at Qilin; he was looking at me with a glint of surprise. Good, I thought, we're both clueless for a change.

Tashi then looked in the direction of our camp and whispered something to his grandmother, who nodded and said to us in heavily accented Mandarin, "I have a message to deliver to the two of you."

We remained silent so she continued. "The person who asked me to pass on this message is Chen Wen-Jin. I'm sure you both know about her. When Chen Wen-Jin asked me to send you the videotapes, she already anticipated that the two of you would end up here. If you reach Tamu-Tuo as her notebook instructed, she will be there waiting for you. However, you're running out of time. If you aren't there in ten more days, she is going in alone. So get a move on, gentlemen."

What the fuck? I thought. Ten more days? Wen-Jin's waiting for us at Tamu-Tuo? I looked at Qilin and was horrified to see that he looked as confused as I felt. But in a second, he was as expressionless as ever. "When did she tell you this?" he asked.

She replied coldly, "I don't need to tell you anything else. There are many people here and some of them may be eavesdropping."

Qilin frowned slightly. "How is she?"

With an unreadable smile, Dingzhu-Zhuoma said, "You'll find out if you make it in time." And she waved her hand at her daughter-in-law to help her into her tent. She turned back suddenly and said, "Oh yes, there's one more thing. She told me to tell you guys that *It* is with you now. You have to be careful."

She went into her tent, leaving Qilin and me to stare at her retreating back.

"What's all this about? What do you know about anything this old witch just told us?"

Qilin didn't answer me. He closed his eyes and started to stand up. I leaped in front of him, hissing, "You're not leaving until you talk to me, damn you."

He sat back down by the fire; looking me in the eye, he asked, "What do you want?

"You know damned well what my questions are—you've been evading them forever. Give me the answers."

He turned his head to look at the fire and replied, "I can't answer you."

"Rot in hell! Why can't you answer? You've been fooling with me repeatedly and you won't even tell me why. What do you think I am?"

"This is my business, why do I have to tell you anything?" He took a gulp of his tea and asked, "Wu, why did you have to follow us? You really shouldn't be involved. The people in this group aren't ones you should even know. Go home."

It was the longest speech I'd ever heard come out of this man; his face was still expressionless despite his burst of volubility.

"I don't really want to be here and my request is simple—tell me what this is all about and I'll leave you in peace. It's only because nobody wants me to know anything that I'm wading in this muddy water."

Qilin looked at me and asked, "Did you ever think about why people have tried to keep you from knowing the truth?"

He fell silent and then continued, "I know why, and I understand the reason. I have many more questions than you do but unlike you, I can't yell at another person to give me the answers I need."

Suddenly I remembered that he had lost his memory in the undersea tomb, and I felt embarrassed for nagging at him for information.

"I am a person with no past and future. Everything that

I've done has been to find the connection between me and the rest of the world, where I came from, why I'm here." He looked at me with a tinge of anger and asked, "Can you imagine being like me, with nobody to care one damn if I ceased to exist? I'd leave without a trace, as though I never was alive in the first place. Sometimes I look at myself in the mirror and wonder if I really am a living being, or am I just someone else's shadow."

"It's not as exaggerated as all that. If you disappeared, I'd care enough to find out where you went and what had become of you."

He shook his head, stood up, and said, "Maybe the day I find the answers I'm looking for, I'll tell you about them. But you won't find the answers to your questions by grabbing me. Everything is a mystery to me right now, too. I think you have enough mysteries of your own to worry about. You don't need any of mine." Then he started to walk away.

"Can you at least tell me one thing?" I called after him.

He stopped, turned around, and looked at me.

"Why did you enter the bronze doors?" I asked.

He thought for a minute and said, "I was following in the footsteps of Wang Canghai."

"What did you see in there?" I asked. "What sort of place lies behind the giant doors?"

He brushed the sand off his clothes as he replied, "I saw the Ultimate—the Ultimate of all things."

He smiled at my puzzled face, and said, "One last thing. Remember, I'm on your side." Then he walked away, leaving me alone on the sand with a splitting headache.

## CHAPTER TWENTY-TWO
# OFF THE TRACK

When we began our trip the next morning, it soon
became clear why the Gobi Desert is called the Land
of Death. When searching for a tomb in the jungle or
under the sea, there's always something close at hand that
will sustain life. Among these wind-eroded rocks and
mountain-high dunes, there was nothing but sand. The
trail we blazed was over terrain that nobody had traveled
for decades—and with good reason. The desolation of the
landscape made everyone miserable, and the heat that
scorched through the air-conditioning of our vehicles didn't
help one bit.

The glare of the sun was making me dizzy; I closed my
eyes and thought of the final message I'd heard the night
before—"*It* is with you now." What or who was "*It*"?

In her notebook, Wen-Jin referred many times to
avoiding "*It's*" search of her over the past twenty years. Why
did she say "*It*" instead of "he" or "she"? Could the "*It*"
that was with us be something inhuman? I shook my head
hard—this wasn't the time or place to fall into this sort of
speculation.

We had reached a dried-up riverbed, which served as
our road. The Qaidam Basin was originally a place where

rivers gathered, flowing from mountain glaciers into this no-man's-land. But climate change in the past centuries had caused them to disappear, leaving rocky, twisting pathways behind. After three days, we reached the end of the riverbed, and in front of us was a small stretch of the Gobi Desert once again.

Dingzhu-Zhuoma said that once we crossed this portion of the desert, we would come to the pass where she and Wen-Jin's team parted ways. It was a spot with odd-looking stones and it looked like a huge gate, so we couldn't miss seeing it. Beyond that was the desert, where ocean and salt marsh had all come together, devouring one another in turn, so the landscape changed from day to day. It was a place upon which even the most experienced guides refused to set foot.

But Ning's team had GPS with them, so they were unconcerned—even though Tashi kept reminding them that their technology could easily let them down.

Then a storm struck. If we had still been in the middle of the desert, it would have swallowed us up and buried us alive but since we were on the edge of the Gobi, the worst it could do would be to create a large dust bowl. Visibility rapidly faded in the howling wind and we had to slacken our speed to a crawl.

The storm went on for half a day with no signs of stopping. We could see nothing and heard only the shrieks of the wind. It was pointless to drive on, since we could easily go off course.

Hans drove the vehicle I was in and he was reluctant to come to a stop. Finally he turned the Land Rover so the sand wouldn't blow into its engine and waited for the storm to pass. It raged around us, shaking us, rattling our locked windows, trapping us in a world of swirling, yellow dust. I could see no lights from the other vehicles; it was as though we two were the only living beings left on the planet.

After ten minutes or so, the wind grew even stronger, pushing the Land Rover and rocking it as though it were going to waft it into the air.

"Have you ever been in a storm like this before?" Hans yelled, a sick look on his face.

"Don't worry," I said. "These vehicles were built to withstand this sort of thing." Then we jolted violently and heard the echo of a loud bang. I tried to look out the back window, sure that we had been hit by another vehicle. But there was nothing—no headlights, no shapes or shadows. Then Hans grabbed me, yelling. I looked out his window and saw something right beside us. It looked like a person, but who would court death by going out in this storm?

It began to fumble at the car door, trying to get inside. As it came up to the window, we could see a face—a man wearing goggles, like the kind Ning's team had. I felt relieved but pissed off. "Who is this jerk?" I asked Hans.

The man began to pound on our window, pointing at the door as though telling us to open it. No way in hell, I thought. Then another person showed up at the other side of the car, also wearing goggles and carrying a flashlight. Both men pounded on the windows and it was plain that they needed help. Hans and I put on our own goggles and heavy jackets to keep the dust from cutting our skin when the wind hurled it against us. Hans grabbed two big flashlights and we opened the doors of our vehicle, heading into the storm.

A wall of dust blew into our Land Rover in an instant, forcing me back inside and blowing Hans on the other side right off his feet. I climbed back out into the storm and realized I was standing on ground far higher than it should have been. I turned the beam of my light toward the vehicle—its tires were half-buried in sand and its chassis was at a thirty-degree angle, sinking slowly into a drift. We were stranded.

One of the men who had alerted us gestured for me to get our gear out of the trunk before it all slipped away from us. He waved into the darkness, and I knew we had to warn the others to come out into the storm before they were buried alive.

Hans and I grabbed our equipment. There was a huge dent in the back of our Land Rover and I looked for the object that had caused it. There was nothing to be seen. Bending my body against the force of the wind, I followed the others into the storm.

Headlights shone through the dust; when we reached them, whoever had been inside the vehicle had already gone. We almost stepped on the men who had left it; one of them had lost his goggles, and his eyes were filled with sand. He screamed with pain as we wrapped a towel around his temples to protect his eyesight from any more injury.

We all moved on. In the next Land Rover, two guys were playing cards as their vehicle sank further into the sand. We had to smash their window with a rock and pull them out by force. By now the wind was so strong it was blowing pebbles through the air; one guy was struck by a flying rock that broke his goggles; another had his nose broken by a projectile. If we didn't find a way to protect ourselves, we were all going to die.

I found a stainless steel lunchbox in my bag and held it in front of my face as a shield, but the wind tore it from my grasp and whisked it out of sight. I dropped to the ground, covering my head with my arms, as though I were on a battlefield.

Then the sky turned bright for a second and something hot whizzed past; three more flashes appeared and I could smell a familiar odor—they were signal flares. Someone was calling for help or was offering us a sanctuary—either way, we had to find where these flares were coming from.

I stood up, and three men who were also uninjured joined me. A rock blew into my shoulder and we all put our bags in front of us to use as shields. Slowly we began to walk toward the flares.

In a few minutes we came across three empty vehicles that were sinking fast. We opened the trunks and grabbed the gear inside, just as another flare went off to our left, not far from where we were standing.

As we walked in the direction of the flare, a huge shape appeared in the whirl of sand. As we drew closer, it looked like a gigantic rock—a great place to take shelter. We raced toward it and soon I saw half a dozen flashlights twinkling through the storm.

But the more I ran, the farther away the lights appeared. What in hell is wrong here? I turned to the others, but there was nobody there. I was alone in the storm.

## CHAPTER TWENTY-THREE
# LOST IN THE STORM

The wind was less ferocious here than it had been; something in front of me was blocking its force. Where in hell were the other guys? I hadn't been running that fast—had they all been struck by rocks? Were they lying injured nearby?

I lifted my flashlight high in the air but saw nothing on the ground. The howl of the wind was all I could hear; for a minute I felt a terrible panic, but knew that was a sure path to death. Forcing my breathing to slow down, I took several deep gasps of air and then moved forward. It was my only choice; if I turned back to find the others we would probably all die. But if the flares meant other people were close by, perhaps we could put together a rescue team.

I jettisoned all the equipment I carried except for essentials and continued to run toward the lights. Still, they remained out of reach no matter how far I ran, and then they began to blur. I fell flat on my face, losing consciousness—and then I felt someone lift me to my feet. As I looked up, there were Qilin and his friend, pulling me away from the lights. I pointed to show them where I'd been going, but there was nothing to see in the darkness.

The lights had disappeared. Even the shape of the big rock was gone.

Qilin and the guy with sunglasses were amazingly strong and carried me with my equipment as though I weighed nothing at all. The guy with sunglasses had a flare gun in one hand, I noticed.

I felt strength return and pulled at them to signal that I could run on my own. They let go of me and I regretted it immediately. They were fast, and following them meant that I needed to use my last bit of strength. We ran for about twenty minutes until we reached the riverbank. By now I could only see their shadows, and then nothing at all.

I cursed loudly and shouted for them to wait; then I stumbled, turned a few somersaults on the ground, and rolled down a slope. Struggling to my feet, I spat out a mouthful of sand. I looked around and saw I was in a deep trench with many other people, all huddled together against the roiling dust and wind-hurtled pebbles.

I was exhausted. A few people came over and pulled me down to the bottom of the trench. Somebody handed me a bottle of water. I could almost hear voices, but my ears were still lost in the memory of the shrieking wind. I took a few sips of water and removed my goggles, wondering why Dingzhu-Zhuoma hadn't known this storm was approaching. Certainly she would know how to survive something like this.

I had read about storms in the desert; some of them could go on for months. If this one did, we would all die.

Qilin and his friend showed up and then went back out to look for more lost men. The rest of us huddled together in silence; few of us said a word. I looked around; there was our guide, her daughter-in-law, and Tashi. I didn't see Ning or Hans, but Wu Laosi was here.

After three hours the storm eased a little, although the wind still howled viciously. Qilin and his buddy brought in more people until even they were exhausted, and we all fell asleep.

When I woke up, the wind was calmer and the only other person awake was Tashi. I walked over to him hoping to get some fresh air. I could hear voices outside and saw some beams of light at the top of the trench.

"Who's that?" I asked Tashi. He handed me a cigarette and said, "Ning is here. The storm is losing force and she wants volunteers to look for the men who are missing."

I grabbed my jacket and goggles, left the trench, and felt much better. The wind had died down and the air was almost clear. I inhaled some fresh air with no sand in it and walked toward the lights and the voices.

A group was examining a vehicle which was stuck sideways in the sand, leaving only the front visible. Ning was holding the radio and anxiously dialing different frequencies.

"What's going on?" I asked.

Someone shook his head and simply answered, "Scattered family."

I didn't quite get what he meant, so I looked over at Ning.

She saw me and smiled, walking toward me. "Just now Dingzhu-Zhuoma said that the storm might come back, so we need to find a shelter as quickly as possible. But all our jeeps are buried, and a few of them are no doubt useless by now. Others probably will need repair before they start running again." She paused and continued, "The most troubling thing is that four people are missing. They could have lost their way when the storm began; we looked around but didn't find them."

"Who were they?"

"Hans and three other guys."

"Hans was with me when he went missing, we were over there. Did you check that area?"

"Yes," Ning replied. "We searched that part thoroughly."

"Don't worry. They all were carrying GPS and the storm was so bad they couldn't have gone too far. It's still dark. Once morning comes, we can look again," I told her.

She bit her lower lip and nodded, but her expression didn't change, and it made me feel like something had really gone wrong. I wasn't familiar with the desert, and I didn't know what might have happened, so I just shut up.

We forced open the trunk of the Land Rover, took out the equipment inside, and moved on to the next. This one had sunk into the riverbed because the ground beneath it had collapsed.

"It's because the surface was a crust of salt, not soil," a man explained when I remarked upon this. "When the river dried up, some spots had more salt than others. The resulting crust of salt couldn't bear the weight of our transport; we stopped in the wrong spot."

Confused, I said, "But we were driving along the riverbed the entire way and nothing happened earlier."

"That's because the riverbed we were traveling along before had been dry for a long time. But this part beneath our feet right now has only been dry for about six months. Didn't you notice that there's almost no grass or shrubbery at all around here?"

"And we're definitely moving upstream on this river," he continued. "There should be a mountain at the end of the bed. If the river didn't change course over time, then there ought to be an ancient city or some ruins nearby. At least that shows that the old Tibetan lady wasn't blindly leading the way. I'd thought all along that she was a liar."

I looked where he was pointing; it looked like there was something at the end of the desert. Recalling the huge shadow I saw in the storm, I somehow felt like it wasn't just an illusion.

That evening, we located all the vehicles and recovered our gear. When dawn came, Ning assigned everyone a task, with some working on auto repair and others launching a search for the missing men.

Those, including me, who had searched for the Land Rovers all night ate something and went off to our own sleeping bags. We slept until sunset.

When we woke up, the wind had completely subsided, and there was no longer any dust. A few vehicles were back in working order and everyone was packed and ready to take off. Ning hadn't slept at all and looked like hell.

"Where are Qilin and his friend?" I asked.

"They're still looking for the four missing guys," she said.

"Do you want me to go out too?"

"Not necessary—three groups have gone out three separate times. Just pack your gear—Tashi and some of the others found a ruined city twelve miles upriver. We're going there because there's going to be another storm tonight."

We had been driving for about twenty minutes when a shadow appeared before us in the setting sun. Soon we saw a huge "castle" emerge in our field of vision.

This was the shelter Tashi had found for us; when we came closer, we found that it was a huge rocky hill that looked like a steamed dumpling. "It's the City of Wind Ghosts," Tashi explained. "When a storm hits this place, the wind sounds as though it's shrieking as it whistles through the rocks, so people believe it's haunted."

It was a peculiar place formed from large rocks carved by the wind, oddly shaped pinnacles sprinkled over a large area. We stopped outside of the "castle," Tashi began to shout directions, and we hurried to set up camp. Sure enough, clouds of sand covered the sky within two hours. The storm continued into midnight and we were treated to a full demonstration of shrieks as the wind torrented through the rocks.

None of us slept much that night and Ning was a complete wreck, obsessing endlessly about the four missing men. I was trying to persuade her to go to bed when we heard someone cry, "Doctor! Doctor! Come quickly! Ah-Kei has turned up."

Ning brightened immediately; Ah-Kei was one of the lost men. We rushed toward the voice who had called to us. It was a guy who had gone out to snap photos; he stood near a pit where Ah-Kei was sprawled at the bottom.

The doctor jumped down, checked Ah-Kei's pulse, and announced, "He's still alive."

Tashi scrambled down to carry Ah-Kei back to camp. I looked at the pit and wondered how this guy ended up here—it was at least twelve miles from where our vehicles had been abandoned and he would have been fighting that deadly wind every step of the way. This was almost unbelievable.

**23. LOST IN THE STORM**

Ah-Kei had fainted from exhaustion, the doctor said, and he soon came to.

"I don't know what happened," he told us as soon as he could speak. "I saw a shadow in the storm and walked and walked without ever reaching it. I fell and that's all I can remember. Did Hans and the other two make it to safety?"

"Were they with you?" Ning demanded.

"They were in front of me. I tried calling them many times but they didn't look back. Now that I think about it, we were walking against the wind, so they couldn't have heard me. Then I fell and fainted. Why? Haven't they shown up yet?"

Surprised, Ning asked, "You mean you saw them right before you fell?"

Ah-Kei nodded. Ning turned to me and said, "Did you hear that? They must have taken shelter somewhere in this place. We have to look for them right now."

We decided that Ning, the doctor, and I should go and look for the missing men. If we didn't return within two hours then the rest of the crew should follow us into the City of Wind Ghosts. We were ready to launch our search when Tashi came over, looking grim. "My grandmother said you can't do this."

"Why not?" Ning asked.

"It's much too dangerous—it's a huge area, about thirty-three square miles, and it's full of sand traps. People have disappeared in this place over the centuries, and you will only add to that number."

Ning shook her head. "You don't have to worry about us. We're carrying GPS. If it's really that dangerous, then we have to go in right now. If we wait until morning, these men may be lost forever."

Before Tashi could argue, Dingzhu-Zhuoma walked toward us. She put her hand on Tashi's arm and spoke harshly to him in Tibetan. He turned pale and muttered, "You're lucky—my grandmother changed her mind. She just told me to lead the three of you into the City."

He gathered his gear, looking reluctant, and the four of us set off.

We walked up a steep slope behind our camp and when we reached the top, Tashi stacked some stones as a marker to give anyone who followed us an indication of our route. "Every time we make a turn, I'll make another stack. If we come across one of those piles of rocks, we'll know we're going in circles," he explained, and we all agreed that was a fine idea.

Soon we entered the City. Black rocky hills surrounded us and I felt as though we were walking through a lunar landscape, dead and eerie. Once we had gone about a mile or two, Ning began yelling into a portable radio while we shouted in hopes that the three missing persons would hear us and respond. In the silent City of Wind Ghosts, our voices broke into echoes that overlapped and faded away at a distance, making us sounding ghostly.

We kept calling as we walked. After almost three hours, we were deep within the City. Our flashlights swept across the rocks around us; we looked until our vision was blurred and shouted until our vocal cords went numb. Still, we didn't see a shadow of Hans or anyone else, and we didn't hear any echoes that responded to our own.

We stopped to rest and Ning asked Tashi how he thought we should conduct the search based on his desert experience.

"This is the only way. We've already gone four and a half miles or so. If our path had been a straight line, we would have come a long distance, but the truth is we've become turned around without knowing it. My compass shows we're heading back out. People are like ants in here, and it's normal to fall into an S-shaped route. I can guarantee only that I can take you guys out safely, but I don't have any advice for finding your missing men. It would be easier if they're staying put. If they're looking for a way out, then what do you think is the probability of two groups of people running into each other in this maze?"

"Have you never lost anyone before?" Ning asked, frowning.

Tashi was stacking another pile of rocks. Without looking up, he replied, "We never come to places like this at night."

Ning and I looked at each other and shrugged. We resumed our search, with Tashi stacking at least thirty more piles of rocks as we went on our way. We had found none of his previous piles, which chilled me. We'd been walking for hours and still the territory we covered was no place we had been before.

Our voices were all beginning to croak so we stopped to rest and have some water. After a brief silence, the doctor suddenly asked, "Could there really be ghosts in this place? Could the men have been taken away by ghosts?"

Coming from a man of science, this question took us all by surprise. Tashi glared at him and barked, "Don't talk like that—of course there are no ghosts. Your men are here somewhere—we just have to keep looking."

We got to our feet, stretching our tired muscles, when a static-blurred voice crackled from Ning's radio. It was clearly a man's voice shouting, but the static was too heavy for us to make out his words.

"They have to be close by if we can pick this up. The rocks would interfere with any long-range transmission," I said, starting to grin.

Ning played with the frequency. The voice grew louder but was still unintelligible. "We're here to rescue you," she spoke into the transmitter. "What's your GPS reading?"

The answer was a stream of inarticulate noise. The interference was strong, but the tone of the person had changed. Obviously he had heard Ning's voice, if not her words.

Ning repeated her message but the voice still was unclear. As I listened, something disturbed me. The person on the other end of the walkie-talkie didn't seem to be talking. The sounds were more like sneering laughter, low and taunting.

## CHAPTER TWENTY-FOUR

# A GHOSTLY CALL

We all stared at each other. "What's going on?' the doctor asked. "Why are they...laughing? What could possibly be funny?"

"Do you think that's happy laughter?" Tashi replied.

Ning looked upset; she stopped speaking but continued to tune the radio, hoping the sound might become clearer. It didn't, but it grew louder and we all leaned forward to listen. It sounded even more like jeering, scornful laughter, almost maniacal. But there were other sounds, weaker noises, behind the laughter. Blended together, the whole thing sounded hellish.

Even Tashi looked worried. "That laughter," he gulped, "it sounds evil."

"Quiet," Ning ordered as she pressed her ear against the transmitter. She shuddered. "That voice doesn't sound human."

"If it isn't human then what else could it be? A ghost?" the doctor asked.

"Listen to this. It's been making the same sound continuously for five minutes. Could you make the same noise for five minutes without stopping for breath?"

"What is it then?"

"It sounds like a robot or as if someone is perhaps scratching on the transmitter with their fingernails like this," Ning scraped at her walkie-talkie with her nails. "But then the noise is changed even more by the constant static."

"Why would they scratch the microphone with their nails?" the doctor asked. "Why don't they just yell, then perhaps we could hear them without the radio?"

"Maybe they can't shout or talk in the place where they are, and this is the only way they can communicate with us," I said.

"Sand drift! They're stuck in quicksand!" Tashi cried out. "Maybe they've sunk so low that only their heads are above ground. Then even the sound of a fart would send them straight to hell."

We nervously got to our feet. Looking around in the darkness, we wondered where those men might be.

"Calm down," Ning told us. "They can send out signals, which means they're safe, for now at least. And the fact that we are receiving these signals also means they're definitely in the vicinity. We might be able to reach them soon."

"We're in such a huge area," the doctor quavered. "How will we find them?"

"Follow me," she said.

We walked and found the signal was strongest deep within the surrounding rocks. We raced through them and came to a high mound that blocked our path. It was a strange half-moon shape, like a giant sail, and we could find no foothold upon it. We were stuck.

Anyone who understands how portable radios work will understand the situation immediately. Like poor signals in mountain valleys, radio signals in this terrain should have been weak. However, when we listened to the radio, the voice was now very clear and it didn't get any weaker. This meant that whatever was broadcasting this signal was in the area of this crescent-shaped mound.

"They're here? Could they have been swallowed up by the sand already?"

"They're still making noise, aren't they? Split up and everybody search," Ning ordered.

We went our separate ways and carefully looked for any tracks on the ground. Soon Tashi called to us. We rushed over and saw some random footprints that weren't ours.

"They were here," Tashi said. "This mound is like a sanctuary; they must have come in here to escape the storm. No winds have entered this spot to erase their footprints."

We followed the tracks; they were very clear on the sandy ground and we could tell that there were three different sets. We trailed them for about forty feet and then the footprints vanished.

"What the hell? Did they go inside the mound?" Tashi asked.

"No! I can't believe this," Ning replied. She looked up at the top of the mound, which was barely visible in the darkness. "They climbed up this thing. Everybody step back right now." She pulled out a signal gun and fired a flare into the sky.

The blazing flame flew into midair, and illuminated the whole area as though the sun had risen. Everything was visible but it took a few seconds for our eyes to adjust to the light. Then we heard Ning scream, "Impossible!"

Under the clear light of the signal flare, we saw a huge object embedded in the mound. It was partially buried with the rest towering over us.

## CHAPTER TWENTY-FIVE

# SHIPWRECK IN A SEA OF SAND

It was difficult to make out exactly what was jutting out in front of us. "Let's climb this thing and get a better look," the doctor yelled.

"Don't be a fool," Tashi snapped. "Give this some thought before rushing into anything. Who knows what could be waiting for us in whatever this is."

"That's right," Ning agreed. "We haven't found our three missing men yet, and we've looked everywhere down here without finding a clue. They're probably somewhere on this thing and it's obvious they can't come to us. We have to be careful. Let me go up there first. If it turns out to be an easy climb, you guys can come up after me."

As she approached the shape, Tashi stopped her. "Don't move. Let me do it. It doesn't make sense for a woman to do something like this. I've climbed mounds like this before, so I'm definitely more experienced." Without waiting for Ning to respond, he held his dagger in his teeth, jumped up onto the mound, and then began climbing up, using his dagger as his pickax.

We watched him climb up to the base of the mysterious object. He found a spot where he could stand firm and signaled us to tell us it wasn't a tough climb. Then he pointed his flashlight to shine on the object.

We could only see his motions, and the object he was illuminating wasn't in our field of vision. Anxious and impatient, the doctor asked, "What is it?"

"I don't know," Tashi's voice floated from above. He scratched his head as he muttered something in Tibetan and then announced, "Shit, this…it looks like a ship. No, it really is one—you guys have to climb up and see this for yourselves, or you'll never believe me."

Ning started her climb before he finished speaking. I was slower on the uptake but followed close behind her. The doctor was too fat; he slipped back down after trying to come up a few steps, so we told him to wait for us on the ground.

We soon were next to Tashi. I squeezed beside him and Ning to see what he had discovered. Under the beams of our flashlights was a wrecked ship, half of it deeply embedded in the mound.

Ning lit a flare and tossed it toward the wreckage, showing us that the hull of the ship had crumbled. In the side near us was a gaping hole that seemed to lead only to emptiness.

Ning climbed to the side of the ship and directed her flashlight into the hole; there in the mud were pieces of pottery. "This looks like a commercial cargo vessel destined for the Western Region, carrying these goods. What a discovery—there are rumored to be thousands of sunken vessels buried in the desert where rivers once flowed—but few have been unearthed. This will make our fortunes."

Suddenly I thought of Hans and the other two guys;

maybe they had seen the ship too and had climbed up to investigate, but where were they now? Could they be inside the ship? Why weren't they calling to us, even if they were for some reason unable to crawl out to meet us?

"Please turn your radio back on," I asked Ning. As soon as she did, a voice rang out from it.

"Turn the radio toward the ship," Tashi urged her. The voice grew louder but still we could hear no words.

"It's coming from inside the ship," Tashi said. "Could those idiots have climbed into the wreckage?"

The hole in the side of the ship was certainly large enough for men to crawl through; we beamed our flashlights into it and shouted. There was nothing to be seen and nobody answered.

"They might have gone inside, but came back out after losing their radio in the ship," Ning said. "Or they may have had some sort of accident inside."

"Then how come that voice is coming from the radio?" I asked Ning.

"We won't find an answer to that until we go inside ourselves," Ning snapped at me. "Let's go, Young Master Wu. Tashi, wait here in case we need your help."

We crawled into the hole; the interior of the ship was full of mud, like a collapsed tunnel. Ning turned on her radio and the noise from it was louder than ever, still sounding like derisive laughter. "What in the hell is making that noise?" she muttered.

Our surroundings were like a trench in a battlefield, a narrow space surrounded by mud. We crawled into the ship's interior slowly, headed toward the sound. It was definitely coming from the innermost part of the vessel.

Ning turned off the radio because we could hear the sound quite clearly without it. We had only gone a few feet when Ning suddenly came to a stop, screaming. I quickly climbed to her side and saw a hole about the size of a kitchen table in the mud-covered wall in front of us.

When I looked in the direction of Ning's gaze, I saw a man half-buried in the space below. It was one of our missing crew members.

His face was ashen and covered with mud; it was impossible to tell whether he was alive or dead—or even who he was. The sound we heard was coming from deep within the mud that he was buried in.

"We found one!" I shouted, but the minute that my voice hit the air, the noise stopped. Immediately I thought about our theory that this noise was an SOS the missing men were sending. It had stopped as soon as I shouted, either because the person making the noise realized rescue was close at hand or else because he had lost consciousness. Either way, we had to rescue whoever was there as quickly as we could.

Ning carefully slid down into the hole. "Stay where you are," she ordered me. "I may need you to rescue me, as well as whoever is down here."

After she climbed down, Ning put her hand on the man's neck to feel his pulse.

"Is he breathing?" I called to her.

She turned her head toward me and shook her head to say the man was dead. Then she began to dig through the mud to free the corpse, which she dragged to one side of the space. Immediately the hand of another body appeared. Ning dug desperately but he was too deeply buried for her to extricate him. I leaped down to help but the minute I touched the icy hand, I knew we were too late.

We managed to pull this corpse to the surface; beneath the body was Hans's pale face. His eyes were dilated and one arm was stretched upward, holding a radio. I pulled him from the mud and Ning felt for a pulse. "He's still alive," she cried. She began to perform CPR, stopping only to say, "Tell Tashi to inform the doctor that we're bringing him an emergency case."

I delivered the message and rapidly returned to find Hans twitching and vomiting. "You take over now," Ning ordered. She took off her outer clothes and wrapped them around Hans to make a sling, with her shirtsleeves as a kind of handle. "Grab these and pull hard," she said as she tossed the sleeves in my direction. I lifted the top half of Hans's body while Ning tugged at his heels. Slowly, between the two of us, we pulled him up and then out of the hole in the side of the ship.

Tashi grabbed Hans immediately and hoisted him onto his back. Carefully he carried him down to the waiting doctor, with Ning and me close behind.

The doctor rushed to begin treatment; when he unbuttoned Hans's shirt, we saw his body was covered with blood. "What in the hell has happened to this man?" the doctor shouted. Hans groaned as we stared at his stomach, which was covered with tiny, bloody holes. There were at least thirty of them all over his belly.

"What caused this?" Tashi asked.

The doctor shook his head and said, "I don't know. Looks like his body was pierced by something like a screwdriver. But why are there no holes in his clothing?"

It took quite a few minutes for the doctor to dress all of these tiny wounds. "We can't carry him out of here until his condition stabilizes," he told us. "We need a tent and a sleeping bag to keep him warm overnight, and we have neither of those things with us."

"I'll go back to our camp and get them," Tashi said. He rushed into the darkness.

I lit a camp stove to help keep us all warm, while the doctor covered Hans with an emergency blanket he had in his pack. I brought out a bottle of whiskey I carried just for moments like these; the desert night was already turning cold and we all were shivering. The doctor continued to care for Hans while Ning and I sat near the stove, both of us dirty and exhausted. Ning looked depressed, which was no small wonder. I didn't know many women who could face what she had in the past few hours. I thought of asking her why she had chosen the work she did but I had to take a leak first. I climbed to the bottom of the mound for a bit of privacy.

As I relieved myself, I suddenly heard a noise from behind a nearby rock, the same jeering laughter we had heard coming from Ning's radio. I whirled to face the sound, wondering if I was hearing things in my exhausted state. I zipped my fly, turned on my flashlight, and walked toward the spot where the noise was coming from. I could see nothing and suddenly all was silent. Deciding it had been my imagination, I climbed back up to where Ning was sitting and soon fell fast asleep.

The sky was already bright when I awoke. I heard Tashi's voice, got up, and saw the entire team had come with him.

All around us were tents and campfires; Hans was safely in his own tent and Ning was still sleeping in a corner.

For the first time, I could see the City of Wind Ghosts in full daylight, and it was spectacular. We were surrounded by huge rocks rising from the ground like pyramids, each with its own strange and distinctive shape. As far as I could see, the landscape held only a profusion of tall rocky spires, and I stared in a daze.

Then I noticed people were removing objects from the gigantic shipwreck. They had constructed a kind of ladder with nails and rope, carrying things out in a basket mounted on a pulley.

Dingzhu-Zhuoma and her daughter-in-law brought me some bread and a cup of butter tea, nourishment that was quite welcome. I wolfed down my breakfast and walked over to ask Wu Laosi what was going on, since he seemed to be in charge of the salvage operations.

"It's complicated, Master Wu. Hans is seriously injured and the doctor isn't sure he's going to make it. We may have to take him to a hospital and we don't want to leave empty-handed, so we're getting some of the cargo off this wrecked ship."

I glanced at what had been carried off so far—the objects closest to me were pottery vessels the size of flush toilets. None of them were broken.

"Where did these things come from?" I asked, and Wu Laosi shook his head.

"Nobody knows. The five-thousand-year-old civilization of the Western Region was swallowed up by the desert long ago, and all of its secrets were buried in sand. But I can say that this pottery we have found is extremely ancient. The few finds that have turned up here have so far all been made of porcelain. Look at this," he pointed to a bird painted on one of the large pieces of pottery, "this strange bird is one of the symbols of the Queen of the West. Her realm was the spiritual center of the Western Region; I believe that is where we are standing right now."

"Are all of these vessels empty?" I asked, moving closer to investigate for myself. Each piece of pottery was sealed with a greenish-black glue that had a familiar spicy scent. I shook one; it was heavy and something moved about inside, but not sloshing as though it was liquid.

"Be careful," Wu Laosi said. "We don't want to open these until we're quite sure the air won't damage what's inside."

Inwardly I snorted; my uncle would never have cared about that and Fats would have already broken into every last one of these things—good thing they didn't come on this expedition. I gulped down the last of my bread and went off to check on Hans.

The two corpses were in the corner of the tent, covered with a large canvas. The doctor was taking Hans's temperature; he looked half-dead himself. "Hans is getting better," he announced as I entered, "but he's still feverish and his speech makes no sense at all. And these bizarre holes on his stomach—look. These dead bodies have the same punctures but in different places; one corpse has them on his chest and the other on his thigh. But there are no holes in their clothes either—I have no idea how these holes were made or even if that was what killed them."

Hans was as pale as a mushroom and his skin was gleaming with sweat. His lips moved but I couldn't understand what he was saying. "He's been speaking for hours," the doctor said, "but I can't understand him either."

I left the tent, looking for a quiet spot where I could try to make some sense of all that had happened in the past day or so. I must have fallen asleep because the next thing I knew somebody was shouting, and I sat up to see Wu Laosi waving at me to come over. He was surrounded by almost everybody in the camp, although I didn't see Ning. There was a strange odor that burned my throat as I drew near, and I covered my nose and mouth.

Some of the pottery vessels were broken. Men were smashing them open and Wu Laosi stood examining what had been inside. About a dozen large balls of dirt protruded from dried, crumbled mud; on them were black fringes of something that looked like hair. As I got closer, I gagged and retched. They were all heads, human heads, and the black fringe was really hair.

## CHAPTER TWENTY-SIX

# THE HEADS OF GHOSTS

Wu Laosi put on gloves, picked up one of the heads, and brushed the mud away from it. The head was very old; I could see its shriveled skin and empty eye sockets.

One of the team compared the diameter of the head and that of the container opening. The skull was large and the opening of the container was small. Apparently the human heads hadn't been packed into the pottery containers.

"This was one of the strange practices of the Queen of the West's people. These must have been slaves from other tribes in the Western Region. Their heads were probably put in these pottery containers when they were children, only about two or three years old. Then they grew into adulthood until no food could be stuffed into the containers, and by that time, their heads couldn't be removed. Then they would be decapitated, these containers were sealed, and the heads were given to the Queen of the West in homage. Her people believed that the slaves' souls, as well as their heads, were presented in the vessels as part of the offering," the man explained.

"Holy shit! Is that evil or what? The Queen of the West wasn't that hideous when she appeared in the novel

*Journey to the West.* In the book she was kind and loving," one of the team interrupted.

"The Queen of the West was turned into an almost maternal legend over the centuries, but in ancient stories, she was like a demon, cruel and inhuman. In those days, rulers couldn't afford to be kind. All in power relied on harsh rituals and claimed to have supernatural powers in order to govern their territories," Wu Laosi explained. "And after all, compared to the slaves who toiled day to day, dying before they turned thirty, it probably seemed an enviable fate to be well fed and idle for fifteen years and then die a quick and painless death."

Wu Laosi began to wash the skull with a solution to preserve it and told the others to get back to work. "As soon as the jeeps are repaired, we'll be on our way," he said. He was interrupted by the scornful laughter that I thought I'd imagined a few hours earlier.

We all stopped dead, staring at each other. We turned in the direction of the sound; it came from the pile of human heads. "Look," someone screamed, "that head is moving!"

It was true—one of the heads was shaking and cracking open as though it were an egg hatching a baby chick. It suddenly broke in half and two red creatures crawled out, each the size of a fingernail. I knew what they were—they were corpse-eating insects. First there were only two, then more and more until the ground was covered with them.

"Stand back," I shouted, "they'll kill you in a heartbeat— they're deadly poison."

It was too late—one of the corpse-eaters flew up onto a man's shoulder. The guy reached out, grabbed it, and shrieked in agony. From his hand, a red rash flowed up his arm and the man screamed as he fell to the ground.

"Don't touch him," I shouted., "If you do, you'll be the next to die. You can't help this guy—we have to kill these insects now."

Men began to squash the bugs underfoot but more crawled out to take the place of the ones that died. Wu Laosi grabbed a toolbox and smashed one of the skulls—it shattered to bits and I saw clinging to the inside something like a honeycomb filled with gray eggs. It was what my uncle had found in the skull when he was first in the undersea tomb. Had his discovery been an incubation spot for corpse-eaters? Did the Queen of the West use these human heads as a breeding ground for these damned insects? Were they her secret weapon? With these insects, who needed nuclear bombs?

"Oh shit, the other skulls are cracking open," someone yelled. People began to run in a wild panic and red flashes whizzed through the air. We're dead, I thought. There was a scream next to me; it was Wu Laosi curled up on the ground, writhing in agony.

Red dots covered the ground and flapping wings filled the air. We had to get out of here as fast as we could—even if our vehicles weren't running, they could shield us from certain death. A couple of men carried Hans from the hospital tent, Tashi had his grandmother on his back, and I went to grab Ning. She awoke screaming and fighting. I struggled with her, yelling, "Trust me for once," and we began to run.

We reached one of Tashi's rock piles at a crossroad and I stopped dead. Only Tashi knew what these markers signified. We had no idea which path to follow. Behind us was the sound of wings in the air and soon a red cloud filled the sky, coming our way. It was time to run, no matter where.

But the cloud followed us, blotting out the sky and filling our ears with its wild buzzing. "Running won't save us," Ning screamed. "We need to find a hiding place fast."

A giant rock the size of a city wall loomed ahead of us; we raced to go around it but it turned out to be a semicircle, a dead end. The red cloud filled the sky directly above us and I realized the corpse-eaters were hunting us down. Desperately I looked for a crack in the rock that might shelter us when I heard Ning shout, "Over here!"

She had found a little indentation in the rock, just large enough for us to huddle into. It was our only hope of survival—I just hoped it came with a lot of luck. We squeezed into it and squatted down; I took off my shirt and held it in front of us like a shield, although not a very good one. Through the fabric, I could see a huge mass of insects descend and buzzing sounds suddenly exploded in the air. Bugs struck the side of the sheltering rock and their creaking wings sounded like volleys of bullets all around us.

I felt as if I were choking and instinctively my body drew back as much as possible into our little refuge. I closed my eyes and waited for death; there was no way out of this trap. My mind was completely blank, no thoughts, no fear.

And then the impossible happened. The sounds of the bugs smashing the rock stopped; the creaking of their wings faded. Then there was silence. Ning and I sat in disbelief and slowly stuck our heads into the air. The

26. THE HEADS OF GHOSTS

corpse-eaters had gone.

"Maybe they weren't chasing us after all," Ning whispered. "Maybe they wanted to take to the sky and we were all going in the same direction. But they could come back; we aren't safe yet." I nodded and we sat still for a few more minutes before we got to our feet and began to move once more. I reached for my water bottle; I didn't have one. In our panic-stricken rush from death, I had brought no water, no coat, nothing for survival. I looked at Ning; she was even worse off. She wore no shirt, only a tank top.

"What in the hell are those bugs? How much do you know about them?" Ning asked me.

"How can I explain these to you? This is only the second time I've seen them, after my introduction to them in the cavern of the blood zombies. In that place, we found one that was red like these and it almost killed us all—today we faced a sky filled with them. I think the Queen of the West bred them as a biological weapon in the vessels of skulls—no wonder she ruled such a vast empire for so long. Meanwhile what really has me worried is I am quite sure we're hopelessly lost in this ghostly city."

We couldn't even see the Gobi Desert from where we stood, and the "streets" of this city were huge expanses leading from rock to rock. If we could only find the desert, perhaps we could follow its edge to the site where we had left our Land Rovers. And we had to do that before nightfall; now it was noon.

We trudged on for hours, trying to memorize rock structures that we passed so we would recognize them if we began to go in circles. Neither of us wanted to admit that we were lost and without water, so we just kept silent.

We were lucky that clouds obscured the blazing sun, but even so, we began to suffer from thirst. Our lips became swollen and our throats burned. After our fourth hour, I was certain we must have reached the edge of the City of Wind Ghosts, but when we looked around our view was still the same: only rocks and more rocks. And yet none of them were familiar so we weren't traveling in circles, which was reassuring. We sped up our pace, licking our lips to get an illusion of water.

Darkness began to fall and the temperature turned chilly when Ning called out, "Stop. We can't go any farther, we definitely can't get out before dark. We don't have a flashlight, and it's all rocky around here, so we can't make a fire. We can only take advantage of the daylight right now before it's completely dark and look for a place to spend the night. Not even the moon will come out tonight; it's going to be pitch-black in this place." She sank to the ground and I followed.

That evening we piled up some rocks, made a stone shelter, and nested there for the night. Ning and I only wore thin clothing and we clung to each other to keep warm without embarrassment. There wasn't a bit of light in this place after darkness fell and we were both afraid of what we couldn't see. We could hear different sounds coming from all around, some seeming very close. We couldn't fall asleep, so we spent the night chatting, talking about why we couldn't find our way out. "In the morning," Ning said, "we should climb one of the higher rocks so we can get our bearings."

The dawn had just broken when we got up to go, both of us in a very bad state. I had never felt this tired before.

I couldn't control my muscles, my vision was blurred, my thirst was intolerable, and I no longer had any saliva left in my mouth. I felt as though we were a couple of ants trapped in a huge sandbox, manipulated by an unseen force.

Hours passed; noontime came. We found a tall outcropping, climbed to the top, and tried to see something more than endless rocks. All we discovered was that we were nowhere near the end of this ghostly city.

Ning and I stared at each other, both of us with the same silent questions. What's going on? Why does it seem like we're stuck in the center of this damned city, no matter how far we go? Could there be some sort of power that's preventing us from getting out of this place?

We looked for a cooler place to rest. There was no point in talking. We both knew what awaited us. We couldn't find our way out, and we didn't have any food or water. After a period of time, we wouldn't even have the strength to walk. We were sure to die here.

I began to think about how long we could live without water—in a cool environment, perhaps as long as three days. We'd already used up a day and a night and our bodies were burning through all the natural fluid we possessed. If we lived for two more days, that would be incredible. Ning must have had the same thoughts because her head drooped and her eyes looked miserable.

Our choice was simple; we had to keep walking. Maybe we'd find our way out or maybe we'd die of dehydration. If we stayed here and didn't walk, we might live for another two days. Death was still the result, no matter what we chose. We looked at each other and nodded as we rose to our feet.

Ning wore a bracelet made of coins; she took it apart, and scattered the coins on the rocks as signs. "If someone comes looking for us, these will guide them to us. At the very least, they'll find our bodies," she said.

We walked for two more days, like moving corpses. Sometimes I felt like I was already dead, flying in the air. Then I'd see Ning staggering in front of me, suffering but still moving forward, and I followed.

Ning was the first to fall. I saw her disappear, then I tripped over something and hit the ground. I had no idea what made me fall. All I could see was the sky, covered with dark clouds. At least without the sun, it will take some time for my body to rot, I told myself, trying to laugh. I wanted to stand up to watch the motion of the clouds, but I had no strength left. My eyelids felt heavier and heavier.

Just before they completely closed, I suddenly saw the sky flash as if lightning had struck. Then everything became quiet and distant as I slowly sank into an infinite abyss. I knew I was dying; it really didn't feel too bad. Or it wouldn't have if something would just stop hitting me in the face, hard and then even harder. I began to rise back to consciousness and the first thing I was aware of was coolness, almost as though I'd been put in a bathtub filled with ice water. Something chilly trickled into my mouth and down my throat. I licked my lips and tasted water.

I thought I could hear familiar voices but sleep overtook me and I passed out again.

When I woke up again, I felt as though I'd been asleep for a long time. My senses slowly returned; I could hear, and when I opened my eyes I could see. There was a big,

26. THE HEADS OF GHOSTS

familiar face grinning at me.

Who is this? I closed my eyes and thought for a moment as I searched in my memories for the faces of the Tibetan drivers. Is it the one who drove the lead Land Rover? No. Is it then the one who drove the vehicle with our water supply? No, not him either.

I couldn't think of who it might be. Then I suddenly realized that this wasn't anybody from the team. This… huh? Fats? I felt the muscles in my brain tighten—Fats Wang? How could he be here? That's impossible—he's gone back to Beijing. Am I having hallucinations?

I opened my eyes again and there was the same familiar face staring at me. I closed my eyes again and thought that this isn't right. It can't be Fats. Even if I were dreaming, I wouldn't dream of him.

I gritted my teeth and opened my eyes for the third time; at this point my consciousness was crystal clear. I looked again and it really was Fats. He had lit a cigarette and was talking to someone behind him. My hearing was still fuzzy and I didn't catch what he said. Then I saw another man's face, also very familiar. It turned out to be Panzi.

What's going on? I frowned. Did I not go into the Gobi Desert after all? Am I still in Hangzhou? Did I dream all of this?

Memories welled up in my mind. We encountered a sandstorm. The Land Rovers broke down. People went missing. The shipwreck embedded in the mound…all of that was very real. It wasn't possible that it was just a fantasy.

At this moment, my hearing returned and I heard Panzi

ask, "Young Master Wu, how are you feeling?"

I tried to sit up and Panzi came over to help me. I took a deep breath as I looked around. We were in a cave with a bonfire blazing nearby. There were some sleeping bags and piles of equipment lying around. It was pitch-dark outside. Clearly it was already evening.

Qilin sat at the edge of the bonfire cooking something. Ning was lying on the other side in a sleeping bag, still not awake.

"What's going on?" I massaged my temples as I asked Panzi. "Why are you guys here? Am I dreaming? Did I die?"

"You didn't die, but you almost did," Fats replied. "If it wasn't for my amazing eyesight, we wouldn't have spotted you guys. You were already reeking of death when we got here."

I saw Fats playing with some coins and knew they were the ones Ning had left behind, but I still wasn't sure how this all fell into place.

"Why are you guys here?" I asked.

"We were following your team the whole time," Panzi said and pointed to Qilin. "Only he knew it, but after you entered the Gobi Desert, we were right behind you. This young lad here had left some signs to guide us to every single spot you camped. So we kept our distance as we trailed after you."

"What? Signs? Behind us...He...?"

Panzi said, "This was Master Three's plan. Qilin and his friend in the sunglasses were sent by Master Three to sneak into Jude Kao's team and find out where they were headed. But nobody expected that you'd get involved. If

26. THE HEADS OF GHOSTS

we had known earlier, Master Three would have told you all of this himself."

I was still feeling confused and it took me a long time to understand what Panzi was saying. "Wait a second...what? My Uncle Three? Are you saying that all this was planned by my Uncle Three? Then...you guys?"

"We were prepared way early on in Golmud. Our team had been putting things in order in Dunhuang for two weeks. When your team set off, we followed behind. When this poker-faced guy left us information that you were in the team, Master Three was shocked. Young Master Wu, didn't your uncle tell you to stop treading in muddy water? Why did you come?"

I took a deep breath and suddenly felt very weak. Shit, I thought. I really didn't expect this would happen. That... that Sunglasses Boy was so protective of me on the way... he was doing it because of my Uncle Three...

Panzi continued, "Master Three was concerned about your safety, so the kid in the sunglasses tried to give you a little help. Jude Kao thought he had outwitted his opponent and gotten rid of Master Three, but he had no idea that we were so well prepared."

"Then where's my Uncle Three?" I looked around but didn't see him.

"Master Three is a little behind us. We split into two groups so we'd be harder to follow. Fats and I took the lead and tracked you guys all the way here. Then we left direction signs for Master Three along the way. But we didn't expect that things would go so wrong."

My mind was completely clear now. I suddenly recalled that night when Qilin said he was on my side and told me not to worry. So it turned out this was what he meant. This was Uncle Three's plan.

"You guys are pretty damned lucky that we followed you the whole time. Otherwise you would have been dried up by now," Fats added. "And you want to be in this line of work with a physique like yours? I think you really ought to go back and tend to your little shop."

"Why is he here?" I asked Panzi.

"What? You don't like me?" Fats blustered. "I was the one who carried you to safety."

I grinned at him, feeling happy for the first time in weeks. I could trust my uncle again. He was on my side, so I didn't have to be on the alert all the time now. And I was used to working with these guys. I knew them. Best of all was that we had Qilin in our corner. I could relax now.

Ning was still motionless. "Is she okay?" I asked Panzi.

"Don't worry. That little girl of yours is in better shape than you are. She's already been wide awake and had a meal. Now you eat something and go back to sleep. You guys only passed out because of dehydration and exhaustion—you're lucky you weren't sunburned. Just drink some saline solution, and you'll sleep better."

"What kind of a cave is this, Panzi? Where are we?"

"We're still in the City of Wind Ghosts; this is a cave that Fats found. Qilin sent us a signal with a mirror and then we all looked for you together while the kid in the sunglasses stayed behind to take care of the rest of the team. It wasn't easy to find you in this place, but the coins left along your trail did the trick. We followed those and found you both lying in the sand."

"We couldn't find our way out of this damned place, but

**26. THE HEADS OF GHOSTS**

we didn't go in circles. I don't know why we couldn't make it out on our own." Then I felt a spurt of fear. "We're still inside the City? Could we still be trapped?"

"We're not as dumb as you guys were. We left signs along the way, so don't worry," Panzi said.

Fats added, "The signs that I left were all rocks this big. You can see them more than half a mile away. And I also figured out why it seems as though you can't get out of here no matter how long you walk."

"Why?"

"This isn't the City of Wind Ghosts—that's at least another ninety miles away. We're in the outskirts, where there are a dozen smaller cities, all connected from end to end by rocky hills, forming a huge chain. You guys were trapped in this chain—how could you possibly get out?"

"The route you took was deliberately designed," Fats continued. "You've been led in the direction created by the designer of the City of Wind Ghosts. Almost every single intersection looks the same, so even if you made a 'wrong' decision at one intersection, you'd still have numerous opportunities to be 'corrected' later. This was a very common tactic used in ancient times."

"You're saying this was created as a deliberate trap?"

Fats nodded. "That's it, but it's not too complicated for somebody as observant as I am. It was probably built as a stockade to defend the Queen of the West; she must have been a student of feng shui to have turned it into something so intricate."

As I listened to him, my mind took a leap of its own. "Panzi, did you say these outer cities made a chain?"

He nodded.

"You don't know, but I have Wen-Jin's journal in my bag. She said the Queen of the West was protected by invisible walls that turned travelers away. A few thousand years ago this place was completely submerged in water that encircled the City like a moat and shielded the Queen of the West. So the middle of this chain should have what we're looking for."

Nobody looked at all impressed; Fats yawned elaborately.

"Am I wrong?"

Panzi smiled as though I were a baby who had just said my first word. "Young Master Wu. We could already guess what you just explained without having to read Wen-Jin's journal. But if things were really that simple, then the ancient city of the Queen of the West would have been discovered long ago. There have been many geological surveys conducted here over time; if the City were that easily discovered, it would be a tourist attraction by now. No, the City of Wind Ghosts is probably buried in sand. We won't just waltz into it."

"So what's the plan?" I asked, trying to hide my chagrin.

"We originally intended to follow Ning's team until we reached the pass where Dingzhu-Zhuoma left Wen-Jin. Then we were going to wait for Master Three and when he arrived, we'd go west to the City."

"But the ancient river course is indistinguishable from the desert sand now," I protested.

"No need to worry about that," Fats said as he pointed to the darkness outside of our cave.

I had no idea what he meant, so I walked toward the cave's entrance. When I reached it, a sudden surge of cold, damp wind blew toward me and I heard a familiar sound. I walked outside into a rainstorm.

"This isn't the rainy season," I said as I stepped back inside. "What's up with this damned storm?"

Panzi said, "Young Master Wu, this rain saved your life—and when it's over it will have filled the riverbed and will lead us on our way. Maybe it's a little gift from the Queen of the West—be grateful."

We rested for two days in the cave until Ning and I regained our strength. We set off on the third day, and trudging through water that reached our ankles, we walked in the rain for another two days before we finally reached the other team members.

"Wait here for your uncle and get your energy back," Panzi suggested, but I insisted on leaving with him and the others.

We drove cautiously through the rocks, with Fats, Panzi, Qilin, Ning, and me all in the same vehicle. The Sunglasses Kid stayed behind to wait for my uncle.

It was a slow and miserable journey. By the end of the second day, we were all ready to stop—but the mountain pass was still eluding us. Suddenly Panzi burst out in a stream of curses and slammed his foot on the brakes. Stretching before us was a steep cliff and below it was a huge basin swirling with fog—there had to be water there.

"It's Wen-Jin's oasis—we found it," I gasped.

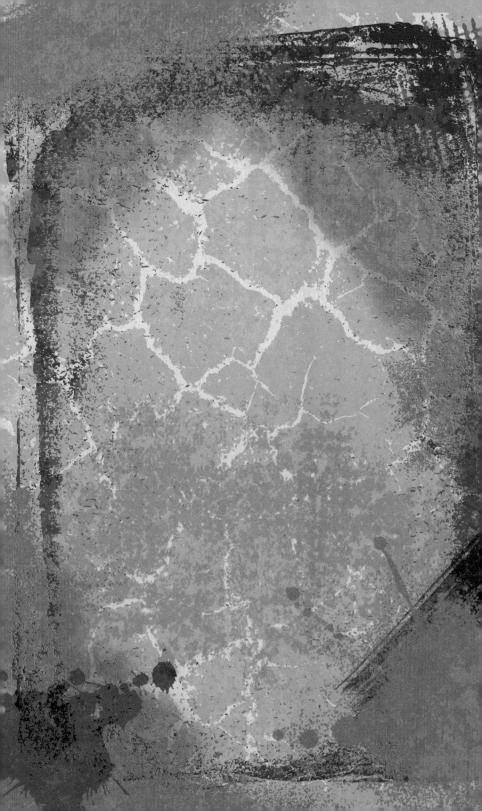

## CHAPTER TWENTY-SEVEN

# MARCHING INTO THE OASIS

The basin was gigantic; looking down from the cliff, we could only see thick mist, and peering through that was a canopy of treetops.

"The mountain pass where Dingzhu-Zhuoma and Wen-Jin separated seems to have disappeared, but there's the oasis where Wen-Jin waits for us. We have to find her now; there's no time to wait for Master Three," Panzi announced.

We got out of the Land Rover, grabbed our gear, and looked for a trail down the cliff. We came across a canyon that led to the basin and began our descent. I pulled out Wen-Jin's notebook and began to feel apprehensive as I read her words; it was a dangerous place, she warned, so humid that the mist was almost a deadly vapor. Within the basin itself was a mammoth swamp that had become a tropical rainforest. Here was the setting of the Empire of the Queen of the West.

Panzi had fought in Vietnam in his youth and was the only one of us who had ever been in a tropical environment, so he would be our leader in this expedition. "We must be very careful," he warned us, "there are going to be malarial mosquitoes, poisonous insects, and blood-sucking leeches. The trees will be so thick that the sun won't pierce through their leaves—we'll be walking in the dark. It will be stiflingly hot but we still have to wear long-sleeved shirts and trousers and boots to keep the insects away. Insect repellent won't help because its scent will attract wild animals—and we have only one gun with us. Most important—don't step in the swamp water or in the mud, if you can avoid it. There are flesh-eating insects and even piranhas in there."

Panzi was right; we'd gone only a few miles before the sky began to darken as we entered the forest. Around us were row upon row of jagged rocks, in forms that looked as though they'd been shaped by an insane sculptor. Tangled roots underfoot made walking difficult and soon we were all sweating as though we were in a steam bath—or a jungle in the Amazon.

Fats wheezed to a stop. Staring into the trees, he asked, "Do you suppose there really are any wild animals in here? We could use some fresh meat to supplement our rations."

"Probably nothing too big, except for snakes," Panzi said.

"Snakes would be okay, as long as they give us some protein. I've had snake soup before and it was pretty good," Fats replied.

"Wen-Jin said in her notebook that there are plenty of snakes here and they aren't afraid of people. Wonder how big they grow in this weird place? It's almost like a Chinese version of the Galapagos—its own little island. Who knows what undiscovered species might turn up here," I speculated.

When I gave it a little more thought, I realized I didn't

want to discover new flora or fauna in this swamp. Legend said the Queen of the West was guarded by a flock of birds with human faces and blue plumage. If they were anything like the birds that had attacked us near the palace in the clouds, it would be better for us if they were now extinct.

It was slow going for us because we had to hack through vines and other vegetation to clear a pathway; it was exhausting and we all fell silent. A ribbon of blue sky traced the tops of the surrounding cliffs and occasionally we passed a waterfall, cascading rapidly after the heavy rainstorm. Then a break in the trees revealed at least a hundred caves on the cliff walls before us. Was this part of the fortification that guarded the City of Wind Ghosts? I shuddered, unsure of what waited for us.

"Let's get a closer look at those," Panzi said, and we walked to the nearest openings. I took out my knife and began to scrape away the moss that covered the cave closest to me. A strange carving appeared on the stone—it was a bird with a human face, carved into the cliff.

It was standing on five skulls; it had two pairs of eyes and a cruel expression on its face.

"It's the same kind of bird that nearly killed the two of us," Fats said. "Look down there."

We stared at the other caves—each one had a similar carving that looked the same as the birds that guarded the palace of doom. We'd all seen how terrible those birds could be and we weren't delighted to discover that they might be here too.

Ning took a deep breath and said, "It looks like the birds of prey that we found in the Changbai Valley are the same as the guardians of the Queen of the West—probably of the same species. The Bronze Door and the Coffin Carried by Nine Dragons in that other valley may somehow be related to the Empire of the Queen of the West—and these birds may have been brought here from the site of our last expedition. Certainly the basin here looks a lot like the one in the Changbai Region."

I agreed. "Maybe that one was the prototype and our dress rehearsal. This could be the real thing and our supreme test."

Fats shook his head and sweat flew off him like water from a wet dog. "Holy shit. You think this is the real home of those damned birds? Then aren't we committing suicide by going any further?"

"Not necessarily. So many centuries have passed, and the climate here has changed dramatically. There's so little food here; those birds might have died out," Ning explained. "The ones we saw in the Changbai Mountains might be the only ones left. But these birds carved here were the guardians of the Queen of the West and finding them proves that we've entered the area of her empire. These carvings are both signposts and warning signals— we need to be very careful from now on."

"That's enough." Qilin broke his silence. "Come on."

We left the caves and plodded into the depths of the canyon. Those damned statues had us all worried; as we went deeper into the forest we knew we were entering a world that none of us understood.

## CHAPTER TWENTY-EIGHT
# THE SECOND STORM

As we went farther into the canyon, the rainforest became thicker, with the twisted roots of trees covering the ground and their leaves obscuring the sky. It was hot and steamy, like walking through a bowl of green soup. Silently we trudged along until the glow that filtered through the leaves faded and disappeared, leaving us in total darkness. Mosquitoes began their ruthless hum as night fell, and then the wind began to blow. Through the dark leaves we could see random flashes of lightning and we knew we were in for another storm.

Then a few drops of rain fell on our faces and a mad patter hit us hard as thunder boomed overhead. The wind gusted and rain blew from the tops of the trees in a heavy curtain, almost painful as it struck us and drenched us to the skin. We put our hands over our heads and raced for the shelter of vines encircling a nearby tree.

An x-ray beam of lightning showed us the canyon as though it were in a spotlight; a waterfall torrented from one of the cliffs, and walls of rain poured from the wind-lashed trees. It was obvious that soon the canyon would be filled with rainwater, forming a river that would rush into the swamps below.

"We have to get off the ground," Panzi yelled. "Come on."

He began to pull himself up the closest tree by clinging to the vines and the rest of us followed—except for Qilin. He was staring at something at the base of the tree, his flashlight beaming upon something I couldn't see.

"What's he doing down there?" I asked Ning, who was the closest one to me.

"I don't know," Ning looked puzzled "I don't understand this friend of yours at all."

"I'm going to find out," I said, and began to clamber down the wet tree trunk, clinging to the sodden vines and hoping they'd keep me from slipping.

When I reached the ground, all I could see was a flashlight. What the hell is he doing? I wondered. Has he run out on us again? Damn this guy—it's as though we don't even exist for him. Then a nearby branch moved and I could see Qilin silhouetted in the darkness, still staring at the ground.

He saw me and beckoned to me to come to him; he had cut away the vines and underbrush, and he was surrounded by a horrible stench. As I came closer, he pulled at a dead vine, exposing the rotting carcass of an animal. Its body had almost completely disintegrated, leaving mostly bones.

Qilin looked down at the skeleton, frowning a little. He pulled out his knife, drew it lightly across his palm, grabbed my sleeve with his wounded hand, and stained my shirt with his blood. Then he reached into the carcass with his bleeding hand and pulled something out of it.

I realized he was giving me the protection afforded by his blood. Although my own had warded off some creatures, it hadn't saved me from the deadly birds and their hideous monkey parasites that had attacked us near the palace in the clouds. What made his blood more powerful than mine and what gave us both this peculiar form of protection?

Qilin was carefully examining what he had recovered from the carcass and I leaned closer to see what it might be. It was a small green object that turned out to be an old-fashioned copper flashlight. Its shell was coated with a green covering and its battery was completely corroded. How did that get inside an animal's stomach in the middle of a deserted swamp?

Qilin reached into the carcass again. He closed his eyes as he probed about and then he began to pull hard on whatever he had found. It was the bone of a human arm.

"This…" I was speechless all of a sudden.

"This creature is a giant tree python that ate a person. The flashlight belongs to that person—and she was a woman."

The arm bone was ornamented with some jewelry and I knew he was right. How many women would have come to this place? Could this be Huo Ling or another of the girls who worked with Wen-Jin?

Qilin was perhaps thinking the same thing. "Go get the others," he told me. "We need them to help us dig up what's left of this python and see who's inside it."

We all gathered around the rotting carcass and began chopping away at the vines that covered it. Soon a large part of the python was in our view; it was the size of a man and within it we could see the shape of a human body.

I leaned against a tree, feeling a bit nauseated. I must have fallen asleep because the next time I looked up, the snake's body was covered with a waterproof tarp and Fats was sound asleep nearby. I glanced at my watch and knew I hadn't slept for very long.

I turned to Panzi. "What did you find? Why didn't you

recover the body?"

"Look at this," he replied, shining a flashlight over the python's bones. "We couldn't take out the body because its bones are so rotten that they would crumble when touched—and we found something else that changed our plans."

I looked at the end of the trail of light and saw something black and rusting in the middle of the python's carcass—it was three grenades that had been tied together and were now fused into one. I froze, not even wanting to breathe.

"Fats found this," Panzi told me. "If not for his incredible eyesight, we would all have been blown sky-high."

"Who was this woman? Why was she carrying this? Anyone from Wen-Jin's team would have been carrying dynamite, not grenades."

"Do you remember when Dingzhu-Zhuoma told us that there had been a tribal separatist group that made their escape into Qaidam in 1993, then went missing and were never seen again after the militia tracked them into the Gobi Desert?" Panzi asked. "I think this body is a member of that group. They probably strayed into these swamps and all died here."

Fats stretched, yawned, and woke up. "Go to sleep, Panzi," I said, "Fats and I can keep watch."

"We should all sleep," he told us. "When morning comes and we can see, we can find a place to make a fire, dry out, and have some breakfast."

But none of us were able to close our eyes and rest immediately; we sat close together, smoked, and talked. Only Qilin slept at first but eventually I dozed off too. I had just fallen into a dream when someone began to shake me back to consciousness. Before I could protest, a hand covered my mouth.

I opened my eyes and saw that it was Ning who was keeping me silent; Panzi was waking Fats up. They both were looking in the same direction and I followed their eyes. A large branch was moving in the wind—but there was no wind. Looking more closely I saw a huge brown python coiling its way down a tree next to the one we were on.

Panzi and the others were all surprisingly calm, not moving or making any sound at all. A python has a long striking distance. With luck it hadn't seen us and none of us wanted to call its attention to our tree.

We remained stone-still as the snake wound its way downward. It stopped, hung its head over a branch, and then looked right at us, its yellow eyes glowing in the dark. Panzi raised his gun and the rest of us backed away, Qilin was holding his knife, ready to attack if necessary. Fats was still asleep.

Could we jump to safety? I wondered, trying to calculate how high we were above the ground. We'd have a better chance of defending ourselves if our feet were planted on solid soil. But of course we wouldn't be on any kind of solidity. The rainstorm had turned the ground beneath our tree into a pool of treacherous black water with roots and vines hidden beneath its surface.

I heard a noise behind me. I turned and there was a smaller python, so close that I could smell it. The others turned to see what had caused the sound and we all stopped breathing.

I was baffled by this; pythons are solitary animals and they are extremely territorial. Except during their mating season, rarely do they join together to hunt. These two pythons seemed to be working in tandem, probably a male and female who had just finished mating. I thought about the human skeleton inside of the snake carcass and felt a rush of nausea. I don't want to be your postfrolic snack, I muttered to myself.

The pythons remained still and Qilin and Panzi both stared into their eyes, motionless as well. It seemed to be a stalemate and after ten minutes the snakes moved to another side of their tree, as though they were ready to give up.

Panzi slowly lowered his gun. Just as we were all ready to relax, Fats suddenly rolled over with a heavy snore that ended in a long squeaking sound. It broke the dead silence and we all recoiled as we heard him.

Ning rushed over to cover his mouth, but it was too late. The entire tree quaked and a wave of stench swept toward us. The python closest to us reared up, its body coiled, and I knew it was poised to attack.

Panzi immediately raised his gun but he was too late; the python hurled itself toward his head. Panzi dodged the attack but when he stepped aside, the fangs landed in Qilin's shoulder. The python slammed its upper body against the snake carcass beneath our feet; the heap of bones crumbled, and the force of its disintegration shook our tree, tumbling us out of our perch.

We were lucky that the vines surrounding the tree broke our fall. I looked up and saw Qilin in the python's grip. His knife was gone and he was struggling helplessly. "Panzi, shoot!" I screamed, but he wasn't in sight and there was no gunfire.

As I stared, Qilin contracted his shoulders and suddenly his entire body shrank. He slid out of the python's embrace, landed on a branch, and slid down the vines to my side. "Get that for me," he yelled, pointing toward a cluster of vines where his knife was caught.

I rushed to get the knife but the python was in front of me

before I could grab it. Its jaws came right toward my face but before it could strike, Qilin hurled a broken branch at it. It moved aside and Qilin yelled, "Jump down now."

Instead I ducked as the snake curled into attack position once again. Then I flew into the air as Qilin kicked me off the tree. I landed heavily on the ground, which fortunately had been softened by the rainfall. Someone pulled me to my feet and dragged me a few feet away—it was Fats, with Ning beside him. Panzi, clutching his rifle, was peering into the trees, trying to find a target.

Then the tree shook as though in an earthquake, Qilin leaped down from it, and a gust of cold wind swept a cloud of leaves toward the ground. Wrapped in the cloud was a massive black shadow that hurtled toward Qilin the instant it hit the ground. He dodged the python's attack and I screamed, "Panzi, shoot that damned thing." Rifle shots sounded before I finished speaking; the snake writhed, coiled for another onslaught, and then sank under a second volley of gunfire.

"Get out of here," Panzi shouted, but before we could move the second snake appeared from its tree, sunk its jaws into Panzi's shoulder, and pulled him up into the branches above. Panzi grabbed his knife and stabbed it into the eye of the python; it loosened its grip and Panzi fell to the ground. Ning raced toward him, her body shielding him from the python, two blazing tree branches in each of her hands. "Grab him and run," she yelled at me.

Fats and I rushed over, helped Panzi up, and began to dash into the woods. We had only gone a few steps when splashes of muddy water cascaded around us. We turned to see that the first python was still alive and had launched another attack on Qilin. The reptile was bleeding from its wounds but was fast enough to have almost caught up with its prey, who was running as fast as he could.

"Hit the ground," Qilin yelled. All of us fell to the mud as the python, still moving fast, crashed into a tree and came to a dazed stop. "I'll kill it!" Fats roared, drawing his knife; I threw myself on him to stop his advance. Qilin crawled over to us, bleeding heavily. "We have to run now," he gasped. "Go."

Fats picked up Panzi, tossing me the rifle, and we began to race into the jungle. We could hear the splashing sounds of the python coming after us but none of us dared to look behind. We used every scrap of strength we had to move as fast as we could; still we could hear the reptile in pursuit. Suddenly Ning screamed "Look—over here!" Under the beam of her flashlight we saw a waterfall, and behind it was a crevice in the side of the cliff.

We ran through the waterfall and squeezed into the narrow shelter in the rock—all of us except Fats. We pulled at him with all our strength but could only squeeze in one of his legs. Ning directed her flashlight outside of the crevice and we could see the python's shadow on the other side of the waterfall. As we stared in silent terror, it turned and went away.

We all looked at each other completely puzzled. Why had it gone? Was it afraid of water? If this snake had come just a bit further, Fats would surely be finished, and we couldn't have stood and watched. It would have been a life-or-death battle. But instead it retreated. Why?

"Listen! Do you hear that sound?" Ning whispered. "Is it the python?"

"No, that clicking noise is here in the crevice—with us," I replied. We all turned slowly and there deep within our sanctuary was a red snake, as thick as my wrist, coiled into an upright position, like a person with no arms or legs. Its eyes were piercing and evil; I stared into them, unable to move.

It looked like a red cockscomb snake, one of the deadliest reptiles in the world. Even other snakes feared it; no wonder our python had retreated.

How could we defend ourselves against this thing? Even if we managed to kill it, its death would only bring more of its own kind to avenge it. All we could do was back away from it and hope it didn't choose to follow. I beckoned to the others to slowly move out of the crevice and cautiously we made it out into the open air. I looked back into the darkness but the snake could no longer be seen.

We all stood by the waterfall while Fats swept the darkness with his flashlight. "No python," he announced. "We're safe."

We began to examine Panzi and Qilin's injuries; Panzi had been hurt only when he fell but Qilin was covered with bloody punctures from the python's fangs. Both men had lost all of their gear in their struggles; the snakes had done more damage to us through that than perhaps anything else.

Near the waterfall the trees were less thick and we could see the sky. It was clear and blue, birdsong greeted the early morning, and everything around us felt oddly peaceful. The tranquility was broken by Fats asking flatly, "Now what do we do?"

Ning walked to the side of the waterfall, held her hands under the cascading water, washed her face, and then replied, "Once the day breaks, we'll go back and retrieve our equipment. Then we'll find a place to rest. It's too dangerous here. We better hurry out as quickly as we can."

Fats said, "What the hell? You do make it sound easy, don't you? We were running about frantically just now—there's no way we can tell where that python's tree was. How are we supposed to find it?"

"We have to go and look. If we don't go now, it'll be impossible to find our gear—and we're going to need it."

I let out a long sigh when I thought about having to go back to the spot where the pythons had been, but the woman was right. We had to do this right now, before we could rest.

We picked up our bags; then a red flicker near the waterfall flashed across the corner of my eye, and I heard that clicking sound again.

"Get away from the waterfall!" I shouted at Ning. She turned and smiled at me just as the snake coiled itself around her neck. Lifting its head high, it made a high-pitched trilling sound. Then it struck. Its fangs plunged into Ning's neck; she shrieked and pulled the snake away. Clapping her hand over her throat, she fell to the ground.

We raced over but the snake leaped up from the water and came flying toward us like an arrow, aimed at Fats. Fats bellowed a curse but wasn't fast enough at pulling out his knife. Just as we all thought he was done for, Qilin leaped into midair and caught the head of the snake with his hand. It coiled around his arm as it tried to escape but Qilin grabbed its neck with his other hand and twisted it hard. Its head swiveled completely around and its eyes clouded over. Qilin tossed it into the water; it thrashed once and then moved no more.

We quickly ran over to Ning. I picked her up in my arms and saw that her face was turning rigid. Her throat moved as if she wanted to talk, and there were tears in her eyes. Then her body turned limp, her head sagged to one side, and I began to tremble. She was dead.

## CHAPTER TWENTY-NINE
# WITHOUT NING

We all stopped breathing for a minute when Ning exhaled for the last time. It seemed impossible that in one instant this brave, stubborn, and unpredictable woman could leave us. We had all been so close to death since we first began working together, and had always escaped it somehow. I'd begun to feel as though we were all oddly invincible. Then with a single snake bite, Ning was dead. It could have happened to any of us—and it might in the next minute. I shuddered and wanted nothing more than to run back to safety, normalcy, and my known world.

Panzi put his hand on my shoulder. "Young Master Wu," he said gently. "This was a terrible accident but we must not let it stop us. There could be more snakes on the way here so we need to leave now. We can stop and think things over when we reach a safer place."

"We can't leave her here," I said, and carried Ning's body while Fats supported Panzi. Walking as though we were in a trance, we silently made our way through the canyon. The sun rose high in the sky and the humidity soared as well; we were all exhausted from the night before and needed a place to rest. We'd reached our limit.

The canyon began to slope downward and the water

that had pooled on the ground after the rainfall suddenly made little rivulets that ran down the incline. Before us was the end of the rocky cliffs and the beginning of black swampland crowded with low-lying, dense green plants.

As we approached the swamp, we saw a large, flat stone protruding from the muck and stagnant water; it was covered with ornate carvings and beneath it was a huge shadow.

"This must mark one of the entrances to the Empire of the Queen of the West," Fats said in great excitement. "We've made it! And look at this, over here."

The shadow was more visible in the spot where Fats stood. Qilin and I looked at it through our binoculars and then stared at each other in disbelief. What lay under the carved rock, covered by swamp water, was a submerged city. Hundreds of collapsed buildings stretched below us under the water.

"Obviously this was once a flourishing city that we're looking at now," Qilin observed. "When the Empire of the Queen of the West collapsed, this city was doubtless abandoned, its drainage system became clogged, and it eventually was covered in trapped rainwater over the centuries. We've made quite a discovery."

"So the queen's palace is underwater too, no doubt," I added. "How are we going to get inside it?"

As I spoke, I remembered that in Wen-Jin's journal she said that Huo Ling had entered the palace back in the 1990s. There was a way in; we just hadn't discovered it yet.

The carved rock was dry, so I put Ning's body into a sleeping bag and laid it on the top of the monument. We all sat down to rest and I stuck my finger into the closest pool.

The water evaporated quickly in the heat, leaving a coating of white powder on my skin. "It's a salt marsh," I said in some surprise and Panzi replied, "Good. That means no leeches and very few biting insects. At last, a bit of luck."

Fats pulled some beef jerky from his bag and that, with tea, was our meal. Then Panzi stood guard while the rest of us fell asleep, knowing we could never go on unless we rested now.

The sky was dark when I woke up and my body felt damp and sticky. It was night and the rain was falling again. Panzi had fallen asleep and Fats and Qilin were motionless. I rummaged around for a lantern in my bag and found a match. Under its light, I took a look around. Something or someone had opened Ning's sleeping bag; her head and shoulders had been covered when we went to sleep but now they were exposed.

# CHAPTER THIRTY

## STRANGE FOOTPRINTS

Who had opened Ning's sleeping bag? Could it have been Panzi? Why would he have done that?

I stood up and looked more closely. Ning's hands were curled in a way they hadn't been when we put her corpse into the sleeping bag. Suddenly I felt frightened.

"Panzi," I called. "Something's wrong here."

He woke up immediately and I beckoned him over. "Did you do this?" I asked.

He shook his head, looking puzzled. Moving closer to Ning's body, he turned on the largest flashlight we had.

The expression Ning had on her face the minute she died was still frozen in place; now it looked frightening. Her body was wet from the rain and the spot on her neck where the snake had sunk its fangs had turned purple. In the heat and humidity, her body was already beginning to decompose.

As we stared under the light, we saw several wet, muddy marks on Ning's clothing. They were still quite damp. Panzi grabbed my arm. "Look at that," he whispered. Near Ning's corpse were tiny marks in the mud that led back to the edge of the swamp.

"Shit," I muttered. "What came out of that water anyway?"

I went to wake up Fats and Qilin while Panzi grabbed his rifle and followed the trail.

I couldn't wake Fats but Qilin was on his feet in a second. I told him what we had seen and we joined Panzi who told us, "I can't see anything in that water—must have come up while we were sleeping. Damn it, I guess I can't fall asleep anymore from now on."

Shining the light on what looked like tiny footprints, Poker-face's expression changed. He quickly swept the flashlight's beam around Ning's body and looked back at us.

"There's only one set of prints. That thing is still somewhere close by," he whispered.

He was right. Panzi aimed his rifle in the direction of Ning's body as Qilin held the flashlight close to the corpse. "Go get Fats," he ordered me.

That was much more difficult a task than it should have been. I shook him, I hit him, but Fats remained in a dead sleep. His face was sweating but when I touched his forehead, I knew he wasn't feverish. I was ready to punch him in the gut when I noticed them—many little muddy markings surrounding the spot where Fats slept.

I called to Qilin and Panzi, who joined me and shook their heads at the sight of the prints. Panzi stood with his rifle in firing position in a spot where he could monitor both Fats and Ning's body at the same time. Qilin handed me his flashlight and pointed it toward Fats. Then he grabbed the knife from my belt and slowly walked over to where Fats was sleeping. He bent down, gesturing for me to bring the light closer. As I did, three small creatures darted out from beneath Fats's shoulders, flickering through the track of light and beyond. We heard the sound of splashing in the swamp water; then more of the same living things emerged from Ning's sleeping bag and headed for the water too. I rushed over to the swamp with my flashlight raised high but all I could see were streaks swimming away from us.

"Were they frogs? Water rats?" I asked.

"No. They're reptiles," Qilin replied. "Look at those marks in the mud. They're not paw marks or footprints. They were made by the bellies of snakes."

"Fats!" I cried. "He's still not awake. Is he all right?" I rushed over and pushed him cautiously, unsure if all the snakes had gone.

He sat up, pale and sweating, looking dazed. "What are you guys staring at me for? I know I'm good-looking but still..."

"We need to check you for snake bites," I said and quickly explained what had happened. He was okay so we walked back to Ning's corpse, staring at the black water that harbored death.

"What the hell is that?" Fats shouted, and we all stared at him. There in the darkness, close to us, was a figure, a human shape, emerging from the swamp. It was covered in mud, standing in waist-deep water, peering at us.

Qilin stared open-mouthed, as though he had lost his mind. He began to run toward the figure, shouting, "It's Chen Wen-Jin!"

# Coming Next:

How could Qilin tell that this ghostly figure was Wen-Jin?
I couldn't decide if it was male or female myself—its face was
completely covered with mud. But still we followed him as he
raced toward the water. Swamp weeds caught at our feet and
plunged us all into the dark, murky pool. Soon the water was
deep enough to cover our heads and we began to swim.

Qilin caught up with his quarry and we came close enough
to see the person we'd been chasing—she was a woman. Qilin
rushed to her side but when he could almost touch her, she
dove deep into the water, heading toward the darkness. As she
disappeared, so did Qilin, swimming in her wake.

Panzi stopped me before I could follow them. "Don't
bother—we'll never find her in that swamp. I don't think even
Qilin will be successful."

"What the hell? Why did she run? Didn't she tell us to meet
her here?" Fats asked.

"Who knows?" Panzi replied. "And who knows if that was
really Wen-Jin."

"What do we do now?" Fats asked. "Qilin is out there in the
darkness without even a flashlight. Should we follow him and
help him if he needs it?"

Qilin needing our help, I snorted silently as Panzi said,
"Probably not. That guy isn't like us—he knows what he's
doing. If we went after him, he'd probably end up having to
rescue us."

For the first time, I wasn't really certain that Qilin did know
what he was doing. Somehow I felt he'd changed since we came

to the swamp but I couldn't put my finger on that difference.

We waited for a while but Qilin didn't return. "Let's not stay here in the water," Fats begged. "Snakes will find us soon and I'm not ready to meet any more of them just yet."

Panzi and I followed him out of the pool and back to the swamp where our fire still flared brightly. We sat near its comfort, and my mind fell into a wild whirl of worries and fears. I knew that without Qilin, we were in bad shape. We had just begun our journey into the swamp and already Ning was dead, snakes had encircled us while we slept, there was a person out there who might or might not be a threat to us, and who knew what would be next? With Qilin behaving more strangely than usual, I was starting to feel as though this ought to be the end of our trail.

Panzi threw more wood on the fire, and the flames shot skyward. I picked up one of our strongest flashlights and turned it toward Ning's sleeping bag; it was oddly flat.

"This is insane," I yelled. "Ning—her body is gone!"

**TO BE CONTINUED...**

# Note from the Author

Back in the days when there was no television or internet and I was still a poor kid, telling stories to other children was my greatest pleasure. My friends thought my stories were a lot of fun, and I decided that someday I would become the best of storytellers.

I wrote a lot of stories trying to make that dream come true, but most of them I put away, unfinished. I completely gave up my dream of being a writer, and like many people, I sat waiting for destiny to tap me on the shoulder.

Although I gave up my dream of being a writer, luckily the dream did not give up on me. When I was 26 years old, my uncle, a merchant who sold Chinese antiques, gave me his journal that was full of short notes he had written over the years. Although fragmentary information can often be quite boring, my uncle's writing inspired me to go back to my abandoned dream. A book about a family of grave robbers began to take shape, a suspenseful novel.... I started to write again....

This is my first story, my first book that became successful beyond all expectations, a best-seller that made me rich. I have no idea how this happened, nor does anybody else; this is probably the biggest mystery of The Grave Robbers' Chronicles. Perhaps as you read the many volumes of this chronicle, you will find out why it has become so popular. I hope you enjoy the adventures you'll encounter with Uncle Three, his nephew and their companions as they roam through a world of zombies, vampires, and corpse-eaters.

Thanks to Albert Wen, Michelle Wong, Janet Brown, Kathy Mok and all my friends who helped publish the English edition of The Grave Robbers' Chronicles.

**Xu Lei** was born in 1982 and graduated from Renmin University of China in 2004. He has held numerous jobs, working as a graphic designer, a computer programmer, and a supplier to the U.S. gaming industry. He is now the owner of an international trading company and lives in Hangzhou, China with his wife and son. Writing isn't his day job, but it is where his heart lies.

THINGSASIAN PRESS  *Experience Asia Through the Eyes of Travelers*

*"To know the road ahead, ask those coming back."*
CHINESE PROVERB

Whether you're a frequent flyer or an armchair traveler, whether you are 5 or 105, whether you want fact, fiction, or photography, ThingsAsian Press has a book for you.

*To Asia With Love* is a series that has provided a new benchmark for travel guidebooks; for children, Asia comes alive with the vivid illustrations and bilingual text of the *Alphabetical World* picture books; cookbooks provide adventurous gourmets with food for thought. Asia's great cities are revealed through the unique viewpoints of their residents in the photographic series, *Lost and Found*. And for readers who just want a good story, ThingsAsian Press offers page-turners—both novels and travel narratives—from China, Vietnam, Thailand, India, and beyond.

With books written by people who know about Asia for people who want to know about Asia, ThingsAsian Press brings the world closer together, one book at a time.

**www.thingsasianpress.com**